# THE WOLF'S TOOTH

*A tale of Liamec*

J. Steven Lamperti

ISBN-13: 978-1-7345974-1-7

Lamprey Publishing
LampreyPublishing@gmail.com

Cover Design by James, GoOnWrite.com

Map by Johnny Quan

Printed in the United States of America

## The Tales of Liamec

*The Wolf's Tooth*
*By the Sea*
*Twilight's Fall*
*The Pirates of Meara*

## The Channeler Trilogy

*Moon & Shadow*
*Sun & Dream*
*Death & Dragon*

*For Claudia, John, and Page,*
*beta readers extraordinaire,*
*and for Andrea,*
*my alpha listener.*

LIAMEC
Ashton
Meara
Lakeside
Brierstock
WESTERN MARCHES
The Dragon River
Capitol
The Serpent's Gorge
BEITER
Grisput
Highlands of Errol
SWORD OF THE SOUTH
The Etenies

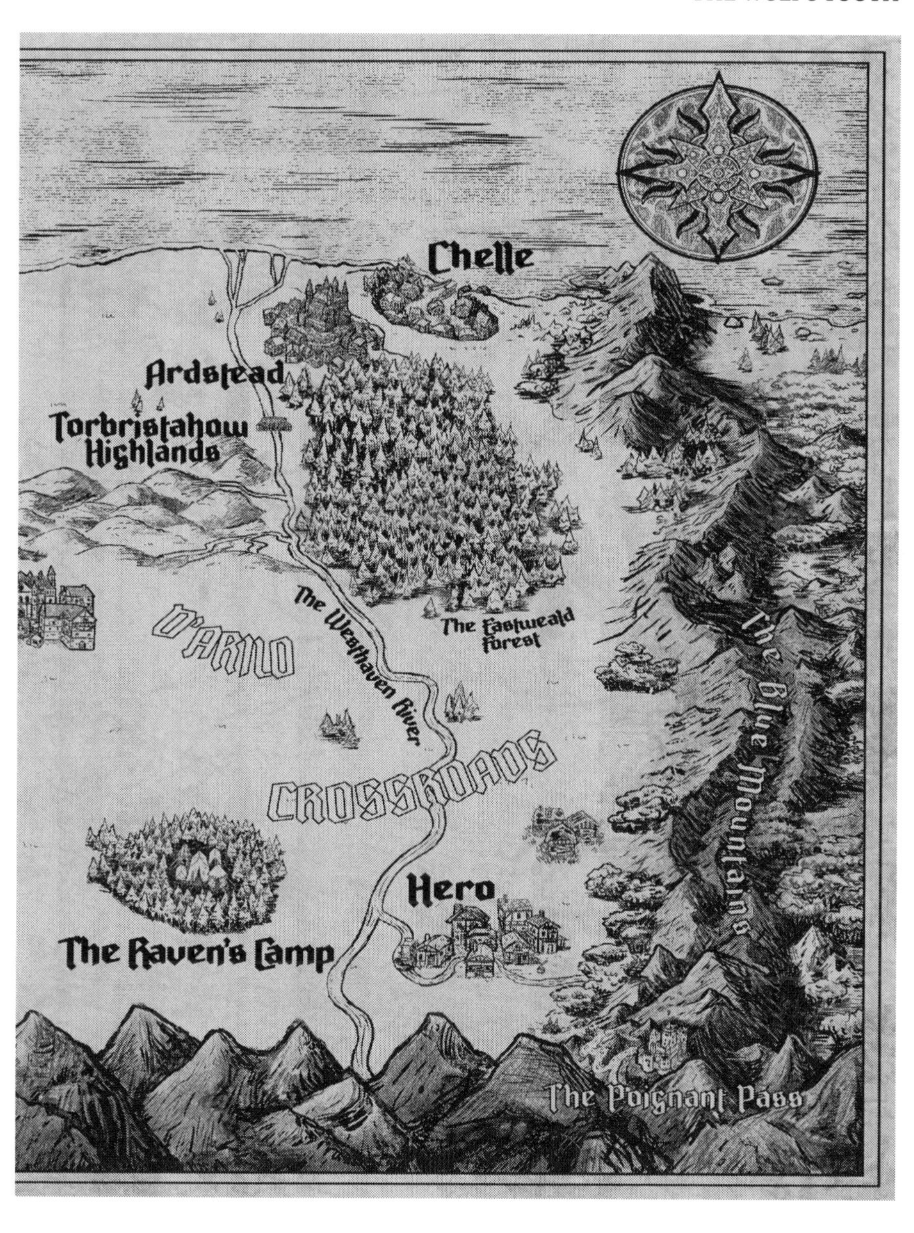
Chelle
Ardstead
Torbristahow Highlands
D'ARNO
The Westhaven River
The Eastweald Forest
CROSSROADS
The Blue Mountains
Hero
The Raven's Camp
The Poignant Pass

# PROLOGUE

There was a land, a country, a state that time forgot, or perhaps never even imagined. A kingdom sheltered on the west and south by the steep peaks known as the Etenies, east by the crags known as the Blue Mountains, and north by the ocean. The state of Liamec was lost to history, lost to time, and later lost to barbarians from the north.

Liamec was large enough to have several cities and towns and small enough to remain unobserved when various destructive historical forces swept through the neighboring lands.

There was a medieval king who had three sons. As his death approached, he bequeathed a third of his kingdom to each of the three. Each was to rule, as king, their portion of his lands. These three kingdoms went on to determine the course of history. They each became influential parts of the foundation of our modern world. At least, that is what our written accounts tell us. What the scribes and historians refuse to reveal to us, hiding the information in their footnotes and addenda, is that there was a fourth son, Liam. Perhaps history refuses to tell us this because Liam, and the king's decisions regarding him, were an embarrassment to both the kingdom and the historians and scribes recording the events.

Liam was an illegitimate child born of one of the king's mistresses. However, The king was fond of this mistress. So as not to wholly disinherit Liam and provide for her, he bequeathed a smaller allowance of land and title to Liam.

This was in the days before magic and mystery left the

world. Perhaps the departure of magic and mystery from the world is what took the names of Liam and Liamec from history's records.

# WOLF

# 1

A baby is walking along a forest path. Well, not really a baby. A little too old to be called a baby, he, for the baby is a he, is just past the age where you would think of him as a baby and just into the age where you could think of him as a toddler.

In fact, he's not precisely walking. The word toddling might apply, but I think a better term might be bumbling. He's bumbling along the path, using the slightly proud, slightly clumsy, slightly bouncy step that makes anyone with any parental instinct feel weak in the knees.

In fact, it's not really a forest. It's just the outskirts of a forest. The early morning sunlight sends bright beams of light shining between branches to glow over the mossy, earthy hillock the path is passing under. It's winding through the moss under a particularly rugged and proud-looking oak tree that stands alone outside the forest. If the boy keeps following it, the path will lead him into the deeper, darker forest ahead, but at the moment, calling it a forest would be a little much.

To be honest, it's not actually a real path. A path implies something built or maintained, perhaps. This is more of a track. An animal track, in fact. If the boy knew anything about tracks, tracking, or animal spoors, he might recognize that. Indeed, if he had that kind of knowledge, he might know that the path is not just an animal track but one frequently used by a wolf pack. But there is no way he can recognize that, as he is just a baby walking along a forest path.

You might expect a toddler walking alone along a forest path, or even a track on the outskirts of a forest, to be sad or upset. This one is not. He is bumbling along like he doesn't have a care in the world. There are other odd things about this toddler. For one thing, he is dressed like a little adult. Leather britches, with the seat proportionally bigger than it might have been, as it seems like there is some kind of tailclout under there. He has an undyed linen shirt on top and a pair of miniature leather boots on his feet. The boots look like they were lovingly made by some unknown cobbler specifically for this pair of small feet.

But there is one more odd thing about how this little child bumbling along this forest outskirts track is dressed. He has a leather belt around his waist with a tiny leather sheath attached. In the sheath is an equally small steel dagger. This dagger doesn't look like a toy. While to an adult, it might be just about the right size to use for picking their teeth, somehow, it seems correct and comfortable belted onto this small child.

For a while, the boy and the track bumble along under the trees on the outskirts of the forest. After a bit, they bumble up next to a gurgling stream that cheerfully joins with the track and starts traveling alongside it. The water in the stream looks fresh, cold, and inviting, and the boy stops his bumbling for a moment to toddle down to the water's edge and take a drink. He has nothing to scoop the water out with and might not know how to do that even if he had, so he just sticks his face into the water and sucks some up. The stream's edge is a little steep, and crouching down to hold his face in the water is awkward, so the boy winds up getting wet. He doesn't seem to mind, and the weather is mild, so he just continues on his way down the track.

The track follows the stream, winding through the trees on the outskirts of the forest, then it finally makes up its mind and dives into the thicker growth. Inside the wood, the mood of the track changes a bit. The beams of sunlight warming the mossy stream banks have more trouble getting through the thick canopy, and the air grows chill with the lack of sunshine. The boy might have regretted getting his clothes wet when taking a drink at the stream if he regretted anything at all. He just continues bumbling cheerfully along his track.

In fact, if he was capable of worry, he might worry about

how well-traveled this track is. It is either traveled by many wolves or perhaps by a smaller number of wolves often.

After traveling along for a time under the dark canopy of trees, the track cuts down under a mossy bank. The trail and the boy round a tree trunk, with the stream still keeping them company. Roots from the tree reach out from the bank to find their way to the stream. Or perhaps, the stream washes the soil off the reaching roots. Either way, tree roots, a mossy bank, and the trunk of an oak tree growing next to the stream cut off the boy's view of the trail until he turns the corner around the tree's base.

The trail cuts across a green clearing. The stream still runs alongside. There is sunlight managing to find its way through the dark canopy for the first time in a while. Relieved to find its way through the trees, the morning sunlight is flooding the green grassy clearing, lighting it, and making the boy blink in the sudden glow.

A wolf pack is watching the boy skeptically across the green grassy clearing. Actually, it's not clear it's really a pack. You probably think of a pack as being more than three wolves. There are only three wolves across the green grass. In fact, it isn't precisely grassy. A portion of the clearing is mossy. Also, it isn't entirely clear. There are low bushes in part of the open space.

Also, the wolves aren't really watching the boy skeptically. It seems they are interested in each other and not aware of him at all. Finally, it's not clear it's right to call them wolves. Wolf pups might be a better way to describe them.

So, three wolf pups are playing in the green moss. The early morning sun is shining down on them. They are rolling and tumbling over each other in a playful, exuberant way. When the boy sees them, the biggest is holding down the smallest while the third looks on. The one on the ground makes a quiet yapping or yipping sound.

The boy steps further into the clearing. The wolves startle, turn toward him, and suddenly look more alert. The larger one takes point, the one on the ground stands up, and they begin moving across the clearing toward the boy.

Now at this point, a couple of things could have happened. If the pups were a little older, they might have viewed the boy as prey and tried to figure out how to treat him as such. If he were a bit older, he might have seen them as a threat and treated them as such. Instead, he walks forward with his hands outstretched and makes a happy sound. The bigger of the wolf pups reaches out his muzzle and sniffs at the outstretched hand.

The pups are fresh out of their den. Like the boy, they are still bumbling when they walk. This is only their second trip out for exploration. The world is as fresh and new to them as any newly born creature. They haven't decided yet that anything in the world is anything other than a toy. So this new toy, this big walking toy, presents itself to them completely unafraid. After a little skepticism, they began to play with it.

Soon, instead of three exuberant wolf pups rolling on the ground and playing in the early morning sun, there are four. The boy seems to fit in immediately. He is willing to wrestle, run, and growl when he needs to. If his teeth aren't as sharp as they should be, he is tough for his size and can do things the pups can't do with his arms and hands.

The boy soon thinks of the largest pup as "Grrr." He is bigger and stronger than his siblings. He certainly thinks of himself as the "alpha" male. It isn't clear they always agree. The boy certainly doesn't.

The youngest pup becomes "Yip." That was the sound he made when the boy first saw him. It is the eager sound he makes when something new happens. He is always curious and always interested in exploration.

The girl pup, middle in both size and age, the boy thinks of as "Sasha." She is the clever one. While Yip or Grrr are sticking their noses into holes and pawing at beehives, she will be sitting with her head on her fore-paws, thinking about smarter ways to do things.

The entrance to their cave is just outside the edge of the

clearing. The pups haven't strayed far yet. These pups and their mother are the sole occupants of the den. She's the reason the trail is as well-traveled as it is.

They are still playing, exploring their clearing, and wrestling when she comes home.

At first, the mother wolf is happy to see the boy there. Her first thought is her pups have been hunting and have caught something. The next feeling which crosses her mind is one of disappointment. *What do they think they are, cats? Wolves don't play with their food.*

The pups haven't seen her yet as she watches them from the shadows at the clearing's edge. She stands there a moment, unsure how to react to this new, unwelcome thing in her world. She pads softly over toward where the four are playing.

When they see her, the pups all come running over to her. Sasha is the first to reach her, and she pushes up against her mother, pressing her back against her mother's side.

The boy comes a little slower. He has established a relationship with the cubs, and he follows his new companions to this new presence. He feels a certain trepidation, which he hadn't felt when he first saw the pups.

She lowers her head as she sees him approach and growls softly. The air around her vibrates with the sound that originates from somewhere low in her belly. The boy stops moving and stands uncertainly a few feet away from the mother wolf.

Yip chooses that moment to bounce in between them. Barking excitedly, in a high-pitched yap, he plows into his mother. She growls again and snaps at him with annoyance but is distracted from the boy.

The morning sun begins to rise into the sky, and rays of sunlight start to flood the clearing. The day is about to fully arrive, and the boy is puzzled as he watches the mother wolf.

Wolves are nocturnal. During the day, the mother wolf will keep her pups safe in their den. In the evening, they will emerge and go about the business of the next night.

She grabs Yip by the scruff of his neck and lifts him awkwardly up into the air. He yelps in protest and then quiets as she starts moving. She heads off toward the den on the side of the clearing.

The mother wolf has dug her den under a tree root on a slope between the stream and the clearing's edge. She widened and deepened an existing hollow. She made it deep enough that the earth would protect it from the weather, and it would be warm from the body warmth of herself and her pups.

Sasha and Grrr go with her as she carries Yip into the den. The boy, unsure at first what to do, follows as well. He doesn't want to lose the company of his new friends.

The wolves all disappear into the den. The boy hesitates, then slowly enters. It's dark inside and close, but he can see just enough with the rays of light lighting the clearing outside.

The mother wolf is lying on the ground against the back earthen wall of the den. The three pups are lying in front of her, nursing or hunting for nipples to start nursing. The boy eases his way forward, goes down on his knees, and crawls up between Yip and Sasha. Grrr growls at him when he gets too close, warning the boy that he better not try to steal his nipple.

The mother wolf watches him skeptically. Still, he has spent enough time with the pups during the day that he smells like them, so though skeptical, she lets him be.

The boy watches Sasha and Yip, then feels the mother wolf's belly for a moment, finds a nipple, and joins in.

Later, when the day set in, the midday sun replaced the morning sun sending its beams into the clearing. The boy woke to the warmth of the cozy den, nestled in between Sasha and Yip, and wondered where he was. Then the soothing rumble of the snoring pups calmed him, and he drifted back off to sleep.

# 2

The boy awoke that evening to the den stirring. The mother wolf had risen early and pushed all the pups out of the cave. The boy started thinking of her as Misha. This evening, Misha treated the boy the same as the other pups. She pushed them all out of the den, got a drink of water at the stream, and set off on her night. The cubs, including the boy, knew their responsibilities for the evening. They included exploring the clearing, perhaps a little of the surrounding forest, and playing fiercely and enthusiastically.

They set to it at once. Grrr, taking his alpha duties seriously, set off to see the exact extent of the clearing. Sasha, Yip, and the boy dove into the responsibility of playfulness.

The late evening sunlight glowed over the mossy slopes beside the stream. The boy, Sasha, and Yip ran up and down the moss-covered hillocks. They rolled down when they lost their footing. The boy couldn't remember having a better time in his life, though his life hadn't been long, and memory hadn't played a big part in it so far.

The three of them were still playing when Grrr returned from his exploration. Running, wrestling, pretending to hunt. The boy impressed his companions by grabbing a low tree branch on the clearing's edge and pulling himself partway up. Yip just looked confused, but Sasha seemed to ponder the implications.

Grrr was in a bad mood when he returned. Perhaps his explorations hadn't gone as well as he hoped. Maybe he had stuck his nose into a hole, and a ground squirrel had scratched or bitten it. Anyway, he didn't seem to be playful when he came back. Instead, he looked angry, and he seemed to want to prove himself.

He started by wrestling Yip to the ground. Yip was smaller than either Sasha or Grrr and couldn't put up much defense. He submitted, turning his head to one side and whining, which the boy immediately recognized as a signal of surrender.

Next, Grrr turned to Sasha. She stood her ground, her head cocked to one side facing him, as she considered how to deal with this threat. Sasha was bright, but Grrr was still bigger and stronger, and soon enough, she was held down on the ground by one of his fore-paws.

It wasn't hard to tell what was coming next. The boy watched as Grrr let Sasha go and turned toward him. The pups were still young, and this would have all looked endearing to an adult human. Still, the boy was also small, and when he stood upright, the pups were about the same size to him as an adult wolf would have been to an adult human. Furthermore, Grrr was in a foul mood, and things felt deadly serious.

The boy stood on a flat mossy spot between the stream and the entrance to the den. He and the other pups had played all night and into the dawn. This early morning was a little windy, and the wind whipped the branches of the trees around the edge of the clearing back and forth. A low moaning sound came from the breeze, squeezing through the branches. The boy braced himself for a charge.

Grrr growled softly, then he paused, peering at the boy. There seemed to be an inevitability to this moment. It was as if this confrontation had been a long time coming, and it would resolve endless unanswered questions. On the other hand, it was just a wolf pup, barely five weeks old, facing a toddler.

Grrr charged. The boy was ready and turned his shoulder to take the brunt of the wolf pup's weight to one side. Grrr wheeled quickly and tried to bite the boy's arm. The boy managed to grab the pup's muzzle with both hands and keep the mouth at bay.

The boy's nose was buried in the fur of the pup's side at one point, and he could smell the acrid scent of the young wolf. Grrr got increasingly irritated. This should have been easy. His inability to get his teeth into the boy frustrated him. As did the boy's refusal to lie down and submit.

The two were rolling on the ground now. Making imprints in the green moss. Usually, while playing, the pups would be careful not to bite too hard. When the cub who received the nip yipped or yelped, that signaled that they were in pain, and it was time to back off. Grrr was angry and not in the mood for such niceties. Also, the boy kept totally silent. The fight had been in complete silence since Grrr's initial growl.

Sasha and Yip stood and watched. Generally, they would have joined in if this were just a playful wrestling match, but they knew there was more to it.

Grrr managed to get a bite onto the boy's leg. Most of what his teeth locked onto was the leather of the boy's britches. However, the sharp ends of his teeth did manage to get through the leather enough to pinch into the boy's flesh. It hurt. With Grrr's teeth locked into the leather of his pant leg, the boy struggled to his feet. He reached to his belt and pulled his dagger from its sheath.

Grrr pulled at the grip he had on the boy's leg. Tugging first to one side, then the other. He pulled hard enough that the boy felt the leather give way. The boy took his dagger and brought it down on the wolf pup's side, holding it in both hands.

There was a mighty yelp, the sound of tearing leather, and the two fell apart. The boy saw a flash of red on Grrr's flank. The pup ran off towards the den, a piece of leather dangling from his mouth.

Grrr and the boy avoided each other for the rest of the afternoon. Sasha, Yip, and the boy resumed their games, but things were a little subdued, and it wasn't as much fun.

Grrr had gained a measure of respect for the boy. Most of his teeth weren't sharp, but he had one which was keener than the rest.

When Misha herded everyone back into the den that morning, Grrr was quieter than usual. She inspected her pups and soon found the wound in Grrr's side. She spent a fair bit of time fussing over him, licking the wound.

Later after they were all done nursing and everyone was asleep, the boy crawled over to where Grrr lay and took his turn trying to clean the wound. He didn't find his tongue worked as well as Misha's for the purpose, but it was adequate, and he felt it helped. As the first bits of moonlight entered the cave, the boy curled up next to Grrr and went to sleep. After that, the boy started thinking of his knife as his tooth.

The next evening Grrr had a new toy. He took the scrap of leather he had torn from the boy's britches and carried it around like a trophy. He would drop it, take a step back, stalk and then pounce on it. One time when he dropped it, Sasha walked over to it to sniff at it. Grrr growled at her, and she backed off.

Later in the night, when he had his fill of playing with his toy, Grrr let Sasha and Yip play with it. The boy didn't find it so appealing. Sasha and Yip also enjoyed carrying the scrap of leather around. They would drop it, hunt it, finally pounce on it, grabbing it in their mouths, then give it the killing shake to make sure they had broken its neck.

Grrr didn't seem to hold the fight they'd had the previous night against the boy. He was in a better mood this evening. It appeared his side didn't hurt him much, though he looked a little stiff the first thing after waking.

He gave the boy a little more respect, though. If he didn't have as many sharp teeth as he should, the one he had was sharp enough.

There wasn't much left of the boy's britches. Later in the night, he lost them, but it didn't matter. The belt and the knife sheath were more durable, and he just tightened the belt a little when most of the rest of the britches fell off.

# 3

Misha, the boy, and the other pups lived in their den and glade for two more weeks. The nights were filled with play in the moonlit clearing, and the days were warm in the cozy cave. The boy forgot or at least didn't think about anything that came before. This was his life, and this was his family.

Sometimes other wolves from the pack came to the den to provide food for the pups or keep an eye on them to make sure they were safe. Initially, they hesitated when faced with the boy, but he smelled right, and the other pups accepted him, so they let him be.

After a while, nursing didn't seem to provide enough nourishment anymore. The pups learned to make Misha, or whichever wolf from the pack took care of them at the moment, regurgitate their stomach's contents to provide for them.

Sasha was the first to figure this out. She licked her mother's muzzle, and Misha expelled the contents of her stomach onto the mossy grass of the clearing.

The pups started eating like they were starving, which, in a way, they were. Their mother's milk had provided for them, but now they needed something more substantial to fill their bellies.

The boy hesitated before partaking. This didn't seem familiar to him and wasn't as natural as for the other pups. Eventually, hunger got the better of him, and he joined in with the cubs.

The rest of the pack lived close to where Misha had established her den. When the boy and the pups played in the clearing at night, they could often hear the wolf pack's howls and calls nearby. The cubs would add their voices to the chorus, though their songs were not yet as strong as the other wolves. The boy also tried, and soon he made passable wolf sounds with the rest of his siblings.

The total pack was five wolves, aside from the three (or four) pups. Misha's mate, Ulmer, the alpha wolf, was the father of the pack. The other three wolves were all younger than Misha. There were two other males and one other female. They took turns coming and helping with the raising of the pups.

During the two weeks they lived in the den, the boy grew to know each of the other adult wolves in the pack, as they each took turns helping to care for the pups. Ash, the other female wolf, was loving and careful with the cubs. When she came to provide food or check on them, the boy was always comforted.

The first of the two young male adults, Kiba was also a welcome presence, though his visits were briefer than Ash's. He was doing his duty before heading back out on the hunt.

Lobo, the final younger male, didn't stop in to check on the pups or provide them with food often. He also never lost his skepticism of the boy. There was no open hostility, but he kept his distance and wouldn't let the boy get too near him. When it was his turn to be the caretaker for the pups, the boy was careful not to upset him.

Ulmer, the alpha, was a stern presence when he was babysitting. The boy and the other pups knew that you limited the playing when he was in charge. Certainly playing on, or near, Ulmer was sure to be rewarded with a nip or a growl.

When the time came to leave the den and clearing which had been home, Misha led the pups to a rendezvous site. This was where the rest of the pack had stayed while the cubs lived in the den. The boy wasn't sure what was going on at first. The cave felt comfortable and safe. Sleeping there during the day and playing and exploring the clearing and surrounding areas felt like the way things should be.

He followed his siblings, of course. The games they played at night evolved. Hunting elements entered the play instead of just wrestling, exploring the clearing, and playing with toys. The boy wasn't as fast as the other pups, but he could do patience and stealth. Misha showed them some things, but the boy mostly learned the hunt's tricks from watching his fellow wolf pups, who instinctively knew how this worked.

In addition to hunting small animals who made the mistake of venturing too near their clearing, the pups started trying to follow the adult wolves when they went on a hunt. Of course, the adults were too fast, and the cubs couldn't keep up for very long, but they were learning.

There was a rendezvous spot not far from their clearing where the pack gathered. The pups set up camp there with the rest of the wolves. Grrr brought his leather patch, which he still carried with him, and kept track of when he wasn't playing with it. The rendezvous site was where the pack had stayed while the pups learned the business of being wolves. It was a larger open space than the den clearing. It was still beside the stream, so they had access to water. Unlike the den, there was no common space where they all slept during the day. Instead, each wolf had a spot under a bush or at the base of a tree. The pups still slept cuddled together for comfort for the moment, but as they grew older, this changed.

The pack lived at the rendezvous site for months, letting the pups grow and learn. At first, the adult wolves still fed the cubs, but they began joining the hunt as they grew.

At first, the pups and the boy had similar experiences when trying to join the adult wolves on the hunt. They all found they couldn't keep up with the adults and would make their way back to the rendezvous site disappointed, only to spend the rest of the night playing and practicing their skills.

After a while, though, the pups began to outdistance the boy. It started with Grrr, who was still the biggest and strongest.

He was the first to leave the pup pack behind while trying to keep up with the hunt. But there came a time when all three pups were doing better at keeping up than the boy.

The boy felt sad the first time he had to find his way back to the rendezvous site unaccompanied. He spent a good part of the night alone, trying to come up with an understanding of what had happened. The boy knew he differed from the other pups, but he didn't want to. He knew the cubs weren't fully part of the hunt yet, but they could keep up with it and see it, and he couldn't.

Having time, while the other wolves were out on the hunt, the boy practiced and developed his own kind of hunting: stealth, patience, and guile. There weren't many animals who hadn't realized the rendezvous site was where the wolves lived, so he had to go afield. He usually picked a different direction than the direction the wolf pack went on their hunt. Not for any particularly good reason, but mainly for his own satisfaction.

The boy hunted more like a cat stalking its prey than a wolf. He would creep quietly through the night until he found a place where smaller animals lived, then wait patiently until a creature thought he was part of the scenery. At that point, the silent stalking and finally the pounce. His tooth came in handy for the kill and for consuming his prey. His jaw wasn't as strong, and his teeth weren't as sharp as the wolves, so he used his knife to cut up and skin the meat.

It filled his heart with pride the first time the wolf pack came back from an unsuccessful hunt, and he could provide his family with a pair of rabbits he had caught.

# 4

As the pups matured and turned into young adult wolves, the boy also grew and turned into whatever he was turning into. As the four developed, the pack size transitioned from five adult wolves and four pups to a large group of nine (or eight, depending on how you count the boy) wolves.

Now, a wolf pack in the wild is a family group. The alpha male and female are not dominant because they are the strongest but because they are the other wolves' parents. Ash, Kiba, and Lobo were Misha and Ulmer's pups from previous years.

The hunting group had turned into a large pack. Five full-sized wolves and three not quite full-sized followed (for as long as the boy could keep up) by a wolf boy or a boy wolf, or whatever he was. Soon, the rendezvous site felt limiting.

Once the pups were old enough, the pack traveled to different rendezvous sites. There were several sites scattered over the wolves' territory. The boy could keep up when they moved from location to location because the wolves traveled with a ground covering lope, not a full-fledged run.

While the new pups were transitioning to adults, Lobo, the oldest of the younger adults, started displaying a temper. He would lash out at his pack members. He showed very little tolerance for the playfulness of the younger wolves.

Sometimes the hunts were group hunts. In the beginning, the pack went out as a group to teach the pups about hunting, but some nights the outings were individual. Lobo didn't come back one night when the wolves returned from their hunt.

There was not much reaction from the rest of the pack. Lobo just wasn't there. The boy felt something was missing and tried to see some signs of emotion in his fellow wolves, but he couldn't find it. Lobo had been distancing himself from the pack, and they had been distancing themselves from him. He and Grrr had been markedly snappy at each other. It was like Grrr was challenging Lobo.

The next night, when Yip and the boy were wrestling to see who was growing stronger faster, they stopped when they heard a sound. It was a lone wolf cry echoing from a distance. The boy recognized Lobo's voice and knew that Lobo was trying to join or create a new home, a new family, a new pack.

That summer was an eternity for the boy, in a good way. There was so much to learn and so much to do and see. The pups and the boy went from being babies to being three young but full-grown wolves and one something else.

The three wolves in his litter and the boy solidified their relationships that summer. Yip became his constant companion. When he wasn't out on a hunt with the wolf pack, Yip and the boy were always together.

Sasha and the boy developed an understanding. They both recognized the intelligence in each other. Both knew the other understood some things the other wolves didn't. Sasha spent some time watching the boy hunt with his patient stalk and pounce methods, and he saw her apply some of the same techniques on her solo hunts.

Grrr was a rival. Most of the time, the wolf and the boy avoided each other, but Grrr still showed his annoyance at the boy when they crossed paths. It seemed Grrr didn't like how the boy fit into his world.

The boy found a way to have a place in the pack. The older wolves still didn't understand him, but they came to accept him. He couldn't go out with them on the big group hunts, as he couldn't keep up, but they allowed his presence. He developed a habit of grooming the more friendly wolves with his hands. He could scratch and stroke in a way that seemed to comfort. After a long hard night, as they were settling down to sleep for the day, he often groomed Misha in this way.

The first winter was hard for the boy. His clothes had long since disintegrated, except for his belt, sheath, and a tattered part of his linen tunic. He soon outgrew his boots, but his feet' soles quickly became as hard as boiled leather. The nocturnal habits of the wolves helped. The nighttime, when it was coldest, was when they were active. Keeping active helped him stay warm. It also helped that the forest and surrounding plains where the pack lived were in a more temperate zone, and the winter never got as cold as it would have in other places.

During the day, when the pack and the boy slept, Yip always stayed near the boy. They formed a bond, and Yip wanted to be close. The wolf also understood that cuddling together was something the boy needed when it was cold.

Unlike the wolves, who just curled up on the ground or on the grass to sleep, the boy soon started nesting. He prepared his own private sleeping spot at each rendezvous site where the wolves would settle, including a pile of leaves or a soft mossy place. He made sure each of his "nests" had enough room for Yip to join him.

Ash left the pack that winter. Like Lobo before her, she found it to be her time to go. They heard her lone wolf howl a few times before she was too far away. The boy and Yip shared their sadness about this. Ash was a loving caretaker for them when they needed it, and they were worried about her.

They needn't have worried, however. A few weeks later, Ash came back to the pack. There was no explanation. She simply returned one dawn when the other wolves came home from the hunt. Ash looked thin and tired. Perhaps she hadn't been able to find any other lone wolves trying to start a pack or any other packs which would let her join.

The pack didn't care, nor did Yip and the boy. They just welcomed her back. Soon it was like she had never left.

Misha returned to her den in the spring and started a new litter. The pack settled into the area around the cave. The roaming they had been doing over the last year was over for a while.

# 5

The boy took his turn babysitting the new pups as all the other wolves did. He loved it. His siblings, especially Grrr and Sasha, had become less playful as they grew. Yip and the boy still played, but the other two took the business of being wolves more earnestly than they did.

The new pups loved to play. They did nothing else.

The morning the new pups first stepped out, the boy was there outside the den. He didn't recognize this himself, but their bouncy bumbling steps were reminiscent of when he first came to the forest.

The new pups were three little gray-brown puffballs of fur. The first cub poked her head carefully out of the den, peering around as if she would recognize something dangerous if she saw it. Another little fuzzy head appeared just below hers, and finally, a third. All three took a moment before taking their first steps into the early morning sunlight.

The sunlight filtered down through the trees into the clearing, just like on the day the boy had first stepped into it. The three pups bumbled out of the den and into the light. They had been learning to walk inside the cave for days, but somehow walking out here in the daylight was more difficult. They took staggering little steps, though each step increased the confidence of the next.

The boy, watching from the edge of the clearing, stepped forward. The pups looked at him warily, but at this point, their eyes weren't working well enough to recognize his difference, and he smelled just fine. Soon they were bouncing around the clearing, over the mossy hillsides, and over the boy with equal abandon.

When Misha came home, too soon for the boy, she

grabbed one of the pups by the scruff of the neck and dragged her back into the den. The boy picked up the next one and deposited him near the entrance. The final pup wobbled after.

Helping take care of the pups became one of the boy's greatest pleasures. When you went to help wasn't an organized thing. You went to help when you felt like it. Sometimes, if Misha needed to do something and needed someone to watch over the pups, she would make a particular sound. It was somewhere between a growl and a whine. One of the nearby wolves would recognize what she needed and go to the pups. Even without this, there was usually someone willing to watch.

The boy watched the pups more often than the other wolves. He caught Misha gazing at him strangely like she thought it was unusual how often he came to help. Still, she seemed to appreciate the assistance and would go off to hunt or on some other errand when he arrived.

The pups loved him. He was more willing to play than the other wolves. They would clamber all over him, crying and whining with delight. He formed a special relationship with one, who he thought of as Skye. She would let him pick her up, and swing her through the air, something the other pups didn't like. She loved it.

There were three pups. Skye was the oldest. Her middle sister was Lana, and the youngest, the male, Nyko.

As the pups grew, they went through the same changes he and his siblings had experienced. Soon enough, they were asking the adult wolves for food more substantial than mothers' milk. They started licking their caretaker's faces to get them to regurgitate their stomach contents. The boy was unsure what to do about this. The first time Skye lapped the side of his face near his mouth, he had no answer for her and felt he had let her down.

He prepared next time. He couldn't regurgitate the contents of his stomach like the other wolves did, which disappointed him and left him feeling a little inadequate. Still, he could solve the problem by other means.

Before going to the pups, he took some meat from the last successful hunt and cut it into bite-sized pieces with his tooth. The knife was worn with use but still sharp enough for the purpose. He chewed on each piece until it was soft enough that he thought the pups could digest it. He then hid this meat near the clearing where the den was located. Worried that one of the other wolves would find and eat it, he hid it on a tree branch. He had figured out that climbing, even into just the lower branches of a tree, was something he could do that the other wolves couldn't.

The next time Skye licked the side of his mouth, he went and got his prepared meal from the tree branch and provided it to Skye and her siblings.

They liked his preparation, which became a highlight of his visits to the den.

The new pups developed quickly, and soon it was time to lead them from the den to the first rendezvous site.

Misha took the lead in bringing the cubs to the rendezvous site, but the boy was there to encourage them. He remembered the change himself and tried to reassure them things would be all right. That the pack would still be with them and support them. The pups were all fine with the change, and it might have been that the boy was trying to encourage himself.

When the new pups turned into young adults and joined the hunt, the boy missed the den and taking care of the cubs. He fell back into his role as a supplemental hunter. When the hunting wolves returned from the hunt empty and hungry, as sometimes happened, they would be relieved to find the boy had something to provide them. The new pups, especially, seemed to expect this.

Skye formed an attachment to the boy and sometimes joined him and Yip in their nest at the various sites where the wolves slept.

That was the fall they lost Ulmer.

# 6

It started, at least for the boy, with a sound. As was his habit, he was stalking near the current sleeping spot for the pack. The rest of the wolves were off hunting. It was one of those nights where the wolves mostly went off individually. Sometimes, even on these nights, a pair might go off together, but usually, they hunted alone. The boy liked these nights better than the nights when they went out collectively. While he would be alone on both kinds of nights, he felt more alone on the nights when everyone else was together.

Yip was still with him. He often stayed with the boy for a while, but eventually, he would be off on his individual hunt.

The sound they heard was a howl. It was distant, as far off as a cry could be heard. It wasn't an everyday sort of howl. There were many howls: the location of prey, the lone wolf, the lost distress call, and more. This was none of these. It was Ulmer. Both the boy and Yip recognized the voice. The cry was distress. It was a wail of pain. It was suffering. Something was very wrong.

Ulmer and the boy had never gotten totally comfortable with each other. Ulmer wasn't exactly close with any of the wolves in the pack. He was a presence; he was the center of the family; he was the alpha. Ulmer and Misha were the ones who decided when to move camp, hunt alone or as a group, or find a new location for the den or rendezvous sites. Not because they were stronger or tougher, though perhaps they were, but because they were the parents, they were the alphas.

Yip was gone like a shot. The boy hardly had time to turn his head before the wolf darted through the underbrush.

The boy took it slower, but he knew he also needed to head to where the howl came from.

He traveled through the night. At first, there were a few similar howls from Ulmer, then they lessened and grew weaker as the night wore on. Then he heard other calls. He recognized the voices of other wolves in the pack and the sounds of grief.

The boy reached the edge of the forest. The open fields beyond felt a little unfamiliar to him, so he hesitated. This was farther from the wolves' territory than he'd ever been. As he stood in the shadow of a tree, the full moon shining down on the open field, he heard another howl. This time, Yip's voice was filled with the grief the boy had heard from the other wolves.

He started across the field.

A cluster of trees near a fence marked the edge of a cow pasture. As the boy entered, he saw a circle of wolves inside the grove surrounding something on the ground.

It was Ulmer. He lay motionless on the ground with his right fore-paw covered in blood and positioned awkwardly. The paw and part of his leg were caught in a steel trap. He had been running when the device closed on his leg. The forward motion had snapped the bone and torn open the flesh.

He had bled to death before the boy arrived. It wasn't clear if any of the wolves reached him before he died, and perhaps it didn't matter.

It was Sasha's turn to howl. The wolves in the circle around their alpha's body were taking turns expressing their grief.

While Sasha poured her heart into her grieving cry, Misha slunk forward to stand next to her mate. She crouched down beside him and began licking at his leg, where it was pinioned by the trap.

The wolves stayed there for a long time. They took turns grieving, with Misha licking at her mate's leg. Eventually, though, the rest of the wolves left one by one. After a while, it was just the boy watching Misha grieve her loss.

The boy took his turn to walk forward. He stepped up next to his mother and slowly laid an arm across her back. He began to caress and massage her in the spot between her shoulder blades, where he had learned she enjoyed being scratched.

## 7

Nothing was the same the next night. When the wolves woke in the early evening hours, they usually looked to Ulmer to lead them, to let them know what to do. His absence was like a knife in the pack's heart. Misha refused to rise. She had slept in a spot under a bush and wouldn't come out. The wolves had lost not just the alpha wolf in the pack but also their father.

The pack splintered. It took a while. For a few months, things seemed to return to something resembling normal. The wolves hunted at night, sometimes together as a pack and sometimes individually. Now young adult wolves, the new pups integrated with the older adults. But everyone felt something wasn't right. That something was missing.

It came to a head that spring when there was no new litter. Without the community's need to take care of a new litter of pups, the pack felt broken.

Ash was the first to leave. She had gone before and so, perhaps, was more comfortable being on her own. She also was the pack member other than Misha and maybe the boy who was most involved with taking care of the pups. Ash left in the late spring. Just about when, if there had been a new litter, the new cubs would have been exploring the world.

They heard her lone wolf howl the first night after she left, but not again after that. This time, she didn't come back. Ash leaving made the boy sad. Aside from Misha, who was, of course, his mother, Ash, had been the most welcoming of the adult wolves when he joined the pack. He missed her.

Kiba followed soon after. He was the oldest of the wolves left, other than Misha. It seemed he was sad to be going, but he felt he had to.

A separation grew among the remaining wolves. Most of the time, Misha was quiet and sad. Two of the three wolves from the most recent litter clung to her and wouldn't leave her side. Lana and Nyko stayed with their mother constantly. Their presence comforted her, and they didn't want to let her grieve alone.

Sasha, Skye, Yip, and the boy kept company with each other more than the other three.

Grrr often kept to himself.

That fall and the following winter were filled with the business of survival. Hunting was a constant occupation that took up plenty of time and distracted the pack from other worries.

In the spring, the second year without a new litter, Grrr left. It was hardly a surprise, and in some ways, the boy was surprised he stayed as long as he did, but it still made the boy sad. Grrr, Sasha, and Yip were his siblings, and he felt a connection to the dispersed wolf that surprised him with its strength.

Another year passed. Again, without a new litter. The boy and the wolves that he was starting to think of as his pack, Sasha, Skye, and Yip, went about the business of being wolves.

Misha's age started to show in the gray hairs on her muzzle. Lana and Nyko were now her faithful companions.

That spring, the three of them left on a hunting expedition one evening and didn't return.

The boy imagined they would form a new pack elsewhere. Perhaps they could join an existing group that was searching for new blood. Misha would always be his mother, but she had never recovered from the loss of her mate.

Late that summer, the boy woke up one evening to Yip, excitedly trying to tell him something. This had happened before. Yip had several times found something interesting on his individual hunt one night and shown it to the boy the next night. Usually, it was something to do with a good hunting location.

This evening was different. Yip led the boy to a site he had found, where it seemed there had been a battle of some kind. It hadn't been a large-scale engagement. If the boy had grown up differently, he might have recognized the king's men's blue uniforms on some of the bodies on the field.

The boy didn't know what to make of the site or what to do with the information. He wandered the field in the moonlight, gazing at the bodies for a time. Eventually, he found one thing which mattered to him and was something he could take from the scene. On one of the bodies, he found a belt with a sheathed knife. It was newer and bigger than his, and the belt was longer. His tooth was worn with use, and his belt barely fit.

# 8

The wolves went about the business of becoming a pack again. It surprised the boy to find his companions treating him as the alpha. When they awoke in the evenings, they looked to him for guidance on the nightly business. He was the one deciding whether they should move on to new locations.

That fall, the pack was back. The mood seemed to have picked up a bit in the group. Yip, the boy, and Skye were feeling playful again. Skye was still young, and Yip had never lost his youthful playfulness. Sasha was the most serious of the remaining wolves. She was relatively sober, even when she was small. Always thinking about and trying to understand things. She seemed to have the most trouble getting over the breakup of her family.

When the pack returned from a hunt one morning, a howl cut through the predawn sky.

It was a lone wolf cry, a lone male wolf.

Usually, a lone wolf will not find a place in an existing pack. The pack is a family structure. The alphas are the breeding pair, the parents. The rest of the wolves are the offspring of the alphas. The ones who haven't matured enough to establish their own packs or have decided that helping raise their younger siblings is enough for them.

This wasn't a standard pack. With the boy as the alpha and no breeding pair, all the wolves knew something was missing.

This was the time of day when the wolves would usually settle down to sleep the day away. Most of them prepared to do so, but Sasha trotted off into the underbrush in the howl's direction.

Sasha was gone that day and most of the next night. Toward the morning, she showed up at the pack sleeping site with a strange wolf in tow.

Sasha meeting a male wolf dispersed from his own pack made sense. Usually, they would pair up and start a new family. In this case, however, seeing as Yip, Skye, and the boy weren't really part of a standard structure, Sasha was trying to bring him back to her pack.

In cases like this, the pack's alphas would usually lead the rest in driving the strange wolf off. Not part of the family, they would not be welcome to join in.

The boy was nominally the alpha of this pack. He didn't have the instincts of a wolf. The other wolves: Skye, Yip, and even Sasha, were looking at him to see how he reacted to this new presence. They would take their cues from him.

Sasha trotted up to the rest of the wolves. The new wolf followed behind her. Every instinct told him and the wolves in the boy's pack that this was strange and unprecedented. The wolf approached with both submissive and challenging body language simultaneously.

He walked forward with his head held low and with his tail down. At the same time, his lips were curled, showing a few teeth, and a soft growling sound emanated from his chest. Sasha kept herself positioned between him and the rest of the wolves. Acting as a living buffer zone to prevent this from going wrong.

The boy wasn't entirely sure he wanted to disarm this situation. He wasn't sure he wanted to change the dynamics of what he had begun to think of as his pack. If he reacted aggressively, the rest of the wolves would respond in kind, and this new wolf would be driven off.

But he could tell this wasn't what Sasha wanted. It also wasn't what was best for his pack.

The boy stepped forward and tried to communicate something non-threatening to the new wolf with his body language. He tried to stay low so as not to intimidate. He put his hands down on the ground and raised his backside, spreading his legs to look playful.

Sasha appreciated his gesture as she came over to him and gently licked his face.

The other wolf looked confused but relaxed his defenses, seeing no immediate threat. The situation disarmed sufficiently that the rest of the pack felt they could get involved. Taking their cues from their alpha, they approached the foreign wolf, and though there was still a bit of skepticism, there was no outright hostility.

Yip, Skye, Sasha, and the boy's pack had grown.

# 9

The new wolf, Flint, had a bit of adjustment to make to work with his new pack. Immediately hitting it off with Sasha helped. Sasha and Flint were showing all the signs of courtship. They hunted together. They rubbed muzzles and made little whining noises. There were public displays of affection. They slept next to each other.

Though it didn't make much sense, the boy felt something akin to jealousy. He and Sasha had always had a bond, born of a feeling of shared intelligence.

Flint quickly joined in the hunt. He was a good hunter and helped supply the wolves with food. Times had been a little lean since the pack had gotten so small.

Sasha's new mate took well to being in a new group. He and Yip and Skye soon adapted to each other, and it wasn't long before it felt like he had always been part of the pack.

He didn't, however, take as well to the boy. Something about the boy bothered him. Perhaps it was the obvious, the fact that the boy was different. But perhaps not. Flint and Sasha were on the path to becoming the mating pair for the pack. The tradition, the instinct, was for the mating couple to be the alphas.

The boy being treated as the alpha of the group was just something that had happened. The main reason the wolves stayed, rather than dispersing, was their attachment to him.

Flint started treating the boy with varying degrees of disdain. Sometimes he would ignore him. He tried to restrict his access to the hunt results. Something which was not too hard as, on long hunts, the boy usually wasn't traveling with the pack.

The prelude to dispersal is often being disrespected or socially dominated. The boy lost his alpha status in one quick moment.

That spring, their little pack had a new litter for the first time in several years. Sasha and Flint led them to the rendezvous site near the den clearing where Sasha and her siblings were born. Sasha cleaned up and dug the den a little deeper. Soon, she gave birth to four pups.

The pack was ecstatic. Purpose had returned. Skye was over at the den trying to help so much that Sasha got annoyed at her and told her off with little growls or nips several times. However, most of the time, the babysitting and pup rearing went well.

The boy resumed cutting strips of meat with his tooth and chewing until they were digestible. The new pups seemed to love this as much as the previous generation.

Flint didn't warm to the boy. When the boy came to replace Flint to help care for the pups, there was often a low growl or irritated whine as a reward.

The new litter grew fast. By that summer, the new pups were turning into young adults. The pack had grown to a respectable size. With summer heading into fall, things were working out well for the wolves.

That's when the world burned.

# 10

It started with a smell in the air-acrid, bitter, and burning. The wolves looked up first. It took the boy a while to register what they were smelling. His nose worked better than the nose of someone who hadn't grown up in the forest, but it was nothing to the wolves.

It was early morning. The pack had returned from hunting. The boy had been doing his local solo hunt and had been successful this night. He was cutting up some rabbit meat. He wiped his tooth on the grass and put it back in its sheath. After his first knife had deteriorated with time, he learned to keep the new one clean.

The wolves, as one, lifted their heads and started sniffing at the air. After a moment, once the boy knew to pay attention to his nose, he also noticed the smell.

The boy didn't recognize the scent right away. He hadn't been exposed to fire in the last few years and had no memory of it from the time before the wolves.

The wolves recognized the smell instinctively and immediately. As one, they all rose to their feet. There was a concerted chorus of whining and whimpering. The pack wasn't sure what to do, but they knew the scent meant they needed to do something.

Once the smell alerted them, it didn't take long to notice something else. A glow showed above the tree line and shone through the trees around the clearing.

The transition from seeing a glow above the trees to the fire being in the clearing was so fast they barely had time to react. The wolves were milling around in the open area of their sleeping territory, whimpering and whining. The trees on one side of the clearing started shooting up sparks. It had been a dry summer, and the fall foliage was ripe for burning.

The wolves bolted, trying desperately to escape the greedy tongues of flame. The fire was coming from one side, so they all started running directly away from it. The pack soon left the boy far behind, though he ran as fast as possible. As with the hunt, his fastest run was slower than the wolves. At one point, he saw Yip turn back and look at him, but there were flames right behind him, and the instinct to run as fast and far as possible overrode everything else.

The boy felt the same loneliness he felt on nights he hunted alone while the rest of the pack hunted together. He also felt inadequate. He lacked in some way. Not only could he not keep up when they were running, but there were so many other things he couldn't do as well as his pack mates.

The boy kept running blindly as directly away from the flames as he could. He hadn't seen which way the pack ran, and he didn't have time to track them. He consoled himself with the knowledge the wolves were staying together. Even the young wolves from the new litter would be fast enough and strong enough to keep up with the rest of the pack.

He, on the other hand, was alone and lost. The fire felt far behind him. He had no idea where the rest of the pack was. He was exhausted and had run through a good part of the day. The boy found a secure spot under a bush and fell soundly asleep.

He awoke with a start. It was warm. Warmer than the day should be. He lifted his head and looked around himself. The sharp smell of smoke filled his nostrils. The fire blazed in a tree not far from where he lay. One problem with being alone was that he didn't have allies to guard him. Someone would have woken them to the threat if he'd been with the pack.

He sprang to his feet and took off running again. The flames were coming after him. They were targeting him.

He burst through some underbrush, out of the forest's tree line, and into a waist-high grassy field.

The field rose away from the forest to a point where it

must dip away, as the boy couldn't see the other side. The flames loved both the open dry grassy field and the slight rise of the land. They were racing after him enthusiastically, roaring and crackling with delight.

The boy ran his heart out, panting and sweating with the heat. As he crossed the edge of the rise, he plummeted off what felt like a cliff, only to collide with a man-mountain.

A crew of men was on the other side of the rise, digging in the soil. They were establishing a firebreak. They had cleared a ten-foot-wide strip of land just on this side of the low grassy slope. The boy came running over the top of the rise, only to fly through the air, arms and legs flailing as he launched off the unexpectedly steep edge of the slope. A collision with the mail-clad chest of the man directing the crew arrested his flight.

As the boy barreled over the edge, the man was saying, "Look lively, you lazy lot. The fire is just about to crest over this rise."

The boy had no way of knowing that the uniform on the obstacle he collided with was the outfit of the king's men. Even if he had known, the knowledge wouldn't have meant anything to him. It was the same gear that had been on some of the bodies on the battlefield Yip had shown him one night years ago.

The man was huge, certainly by the boy's standards. He wore a full chain mail suit, including a blue tabard emblazoned with a black silhouette of a lion's head.

He caught the boy before he could bounce off. The man barely seemed to notice the impact. He held the boy by his belt and his hair-the only things available to grab onto.

"What have we here?" he said.

The boy was frantic. Something was stopping him from running from the fire. Also, he couldn't get free, and the grip on his hair was extremely painful. He pulled his tooth from his belt and stabbed it into the man's chest with all his might.

The blade snapped off. There was a cut in the tabard but not a trace of penetration of the chain mail. The man released his grip on the boy's hair, keeping hold of the belt, and struck the boy on the head with one heavy chain-mailed hand. As he did so, he said, "I don't have time for this."

The world went black.

# 11

The boy awoke with a massive headache. For a moment, as he opened his eyes, everything looked blurry. It didn't get better when things settled. Where were the stars? It was night, but he couldn't see the sky.

He tried to move, to get up, but he found he couldn't. His hands were behind him at an awkward angle, and he couldn't move them or his feet. He cried out and gave a whine of frustration.

"You're awake at last," said a voice. "Someone to talk to."

Something was wrong with the voice. It wasn't just that the boy didn't understand what was said. There was also something wrong with the way it sounded.

"Are you all right? How's your head?"

The boy figured out what was wrong with the voice. It was like when Sasha pretended to be mad at her pups. She would growl at them and make all the sounds of anger, but the sounds were just pretending. If you listened carefully, you could hear she didn't mean it.

This voice, too, was pretending something. It was false, somehow.

"Hey, boy," the voice insisted, "say something."

The boy looked around. The stars weren't missing; it was some kind of den. It was dark, but the boy was used to the dark. He had spent years coping with the fact he couldn't see as well as the rest of his pack. He was well trained to do things in the darkness.

The den was oddly shaped and had high ceilings. He lay on the ground in one corner. He twisted his body and saw who was making noises.

"The guards will come in to feed us at some point, I would

imagine," the voice said. "I hope they untie us. We're locked in a cell. I don't see any point in them leaving us tied up."

The person lay on the ground like the boy. The boy saw leather thongs around the person's ankles and wrists and thought he understood why he was having trouble moving.

He also figured out something about the sound of the voice. Like when Sasha pretended to be angry with her pups, this voice was trying to sound more aggressive. It was lower than it would naturally be. The person was making their voice sound lower than it should.

The person was clad all in leather. Light armor, enough to protect a little in a fight, but not enough to slow you down. Smaller than the man-mountain the boy had collided with, but still larger than the boy. The boy was, after all, just a child.

"Is there something wrong with you? Why won't you answer me?"

The boy could see the sky. If he twisted his head a certain way and looked up, there was an opening, and he could see one star.

"My name is Arnie," said the voice, sounding even a little deeper while saying this. "What's yours?"

The boy struggled with his bonds, but it was hopeless. He could tell they were too strong.

The voice dropped lower and, in a conspiratorial tone, said, "Don't worry. I'm with the Raven. He won't leave us locked up in here. He'll send someone to rescue us."

The boy wished his companion in misfortune would stop whimpering. It was getting a little sad. He was exhausted. Eventually, he dropped off to sleep even with the inability to move, the hard floor, and the awkward position.

Arnie tried to talk to the boy a few more times but gradually realized he was sleeping and gave up.

The boy awoke later to sounds coming from the window. It was a small high window with vertical iron bars across it.

Another voice whispered into the room, a different one

than Arnie's. This voice was even deeper than Arnie's, but the depth seemed fitting this time.

"Anne," it said. "You in there?"

There was a gasp from the other occupant of the room. "Bear! Is that you?" The voice sounded completely different this time. The fake depth was gone.

"Yeah, it's me. Give me just a minute, and I'll get you out of there."

"What are you going to do with the bars?"

"Oscar gave me something. Just a minute."

"I'm tied up in here. I won't be able to get out."

"There's no way I can fit through this window, even without the bars," said the voice identified as Bear. "I brought Jordan. I'll send him in." The tone was a deep rumbling sound, like the roar of distant thunder. It was much deeper than the artificial depth in Arnie's voice. It sent a reverberation through the room each time Bear spoke.

There were some sounds. Popping and sizzling. Bear said at one point, "Oscar told me to be careful not to touch this stuff, so I'm trying to be careful. Just a minute."

Eventually, the sizzling stopped, and there were a series of muffled clangs. One for each bar as it was forced out of the window.

A dark shape passed between the boy and the star he had seen.

"Jordan," said Anne's voice, with no trace of the fake depth. "Get these things off me."

The boy could hear sounds as someone cut the leather thongs binding his companion. Then in the dim light, he saw her half stand and rub at her ankles and wrists.

"I want to take him too," said Anne.

"Who is he?" said a voice the boy hadn't heard before.

"I don't know, but I feel sorry for him, and if the regent's men want him, then we don't want them to have him."

The person identified as Jordan came over and stood over the boy. He was even smaller than Anne, and the boy got the feeling of youth from his voice.

"He's naked, filthy, and he stinks," he said.

"Don't untie him," said Anne, "I think there's something wrong with him."

Jordan reached down toward the boy. A snapping sound was followed by a muffled cry of pain.

"Jesus's whiskers!" Jordan said. "He bit me."

"I told you, I think there's something wrong with him. Hand him out to Bear, carefully."

# RAVEN

# 1

The boy lay on a less painful surface now. Bear and Jordan had deposited him on a soft spot in a new den. The roof of this one wasn't as solid-looking as the roof in the last one. This one seemed to move with the wind he could hear outside.

Bear had carried the boy for a long time. He had lifted the boy effortlessly. Of course, the boy didn't weigh much. Even less so, as he hadn't eaten in days. He was increasingly aware of how hungry he was.

At first, the boy tried to bite and snarl at Bear, but he stopped after a while when he realized how little effect it had. Bear carried him slung over one of his shoulders. The boy's face was pressed up against the big man's back. Bear didn't have an unpleasant scent, though it was a very unfamiliar smell to the boy. A bit of sweat, as he had worked through the night, but under that, he smelled clean.

They arrived at a large camp just as the morning light broke. People were beginning to rise and come out of the tents and wooden buildings as Bear, Jordan, and Anne walked into the site. Several people greeted Anne enthusiastically and came over to talk to her. Bear just kept on walking. He called out to Anne as he moved on. "Anne, the Raven will want to talk to us. I'll meet you over at his tent. I'm just going to put this stuff down."

Bear and Jordan dropped the boy off in one of the tents. It was a large canvas roofed wooden structure on a raised wooden platform. It looked permanent. Not as fixed, perhaps, as a structure with a more solid roof, but it wasn't going anywhere.

Bear dropped the boy unceremoniously onto the cot in one corner of the room. He looked at Jordan and said, "We'll figure out what to do with him later. Right now, we need to let the Raven know how things went."

Left to his own devices, the boy struggled with his bonds again. At one point, Anne and Jordan had loosened them so they wouldn't cut off his circulation. They seemed to know what they were doing. While they were loose enough to not be uncomfortable, he still didn't have any luck getting free.

He looked around the room, trying to get his bearings. What he saw didn't make much sense to him, but he attempted to understand it in his own context.

Rough wood walled the room, and it was roofed with canvas. It might have been someone's private room in the camp. Perhaps Bear's, as that was who had dropped him here.

There weren't any personal things in the room, just some rough wooden furniture and the cot the boy lay on.

There was not much for the boy to do but contemplate how hungry he was until his captors returned.

The boy heard voices outside the door.

"Oscar," he heard a voice he recognized immediately as the voice of Bear. "I meant to thank you for the potion or whatever it was you gave me. It worked a treat on those iron bars."

The door opened, and three people entered the room.

"No problem," said one of them, "part of the job."

It was Anne, Bear, and this new one must be Oscar. The boy recognized Anne and Bear by their smells.

Anne had changed. She no longer wore the light leathers. Now she was dressed in a linen smock dyed a light blue. To anyone other than the boy, it would have been hard to mistake her for a man now.

Bear still wore the leathers he was wearing the night before. He was a huge man. It would have been a close contest whether he or the man-mountain the boy had collided with was bigger. Bear had a full beard. Brown and curly, like the hair on his head.

The third person, Oscar, was dressed in a patchwork shirt of linen squares, dyed all different colors. It must have been dazzling once, but the colors had faded, making them all different shades of pastels. He looked a little older than the other two. They were both, probably, of a similar age. Somewhere in their mid to late twenties or so. Oscar might be something like a decade older.

Oscar shaved his beard into vertical strips. A band of beard from each side-burn, a shaved patch between them, and another stripe down the middle.

"The Raven wasn't impressed with how I pretended to be a man," said Anne. Her voice sounded disappointed. "I thought it was clever."

"He was worried about you," said Bear. "We all were."

"So," said Oscar, inspecting the boy. "What have we here? He's just as filthy as you described him, but I thought he'd look more animal-like. He's just a dirty little boy."

Sensing they were talking about him, the boy snarled, growled, and then gave up with a whimper.

Anne held a bowl of something in her hands. The scent everyone else recognized as stew smelled like meat and food to the boy. It felt like heaven. It was probably the source of the whimper.

"Hold him up. Careful, he bites," Anne said to the other two.

Bear and Oscar sat down on both sides of the boy on the cot and raised him to a sitting position.

Anne carefully, keeping her distance so as not to get bitten, spooned some stew into the boy's mouth. His initial reaction was to resist and keep his mouth closed. The spoonful of meat and vegetables under his nose made it impossible.

Anne gave him a few bites and then leaned over to put the bowl on the ground.

"We probably shouldn't give him too much at first," she said. "Who knows how empty his stomach is."

As she leaned past the boy to place the bowl down, he

craned his head toward her. Oscar and Bear both reacted quickly. Bear called out, “Look out!”

They reacted too slowly. The boy reached out his neck, opened his mouth, and licked Anne on the cheek.

# 2

Anne adopted the boy as a pet. The first priorities were figuring out how to get him cleaned up and get some clothes on him. In the beginning, she used the expedient of having two people hold him as she did whatever else needed to be done. Using this method, she gave him a bath, cut his hair (basically shaved his head, there wasn't much to be saved), and got him into some pants.

She kept him tied up at this point. He still seemed inclined to snap and bite and showed no signs of speaking or understanding speech.

Bear and Oscar were curious about the whole process. Bear felt connected to the boy after being the one who had saved him and carried him to camp. Oscar seemed to feel some scientific curiosity. After the cleanup, the three of them examined him to see if his lack of speech was due to ignorance or inability.

They propped the cleaned-up boy on one side of a table in one of the tent rooms, and the three of them sat on the other side like a review board. They freed his hands for the first time to establish some trust. Bear argued it was still dangerous, but Anne pointed out both he and Oscar were there to help, and after all, it was just a little boy they were talking about.

"Alright," said Oscar, "how should we do this? Perhaps you should do the talking, Anne. He seems to respond to you."

Anne looked at the boy. He stared back at her. He had stopped growling and snarling, for the most part, but hadn't said anything which resembled human speech.

"Maybe his family lost him in the woods?" said Bear.

Anne didn't think there was anything wrong with his brain. He seemed to respond to things intelligently, just not the way she would expect.

She decided to try some basics.

"What's your name?" She said calmly, trying to meet the boy's eyes. She repeated the word 'name' a few times.

She held her hand to her chest and said with deliberation, "My name is Anne. Anne."

What she thought was an intelligent look in his eyes encouraged her.

"Oscar," she said, pointing at the older man.

"Arturo," she said, pointing at Bear.

"Bear," Bear said firmly.

"What's your name?" she repeated, pointing again at the boy.

The boy seemed to struggle. He snarled, baring his teeth. Then, he opened his mouth, spitting and strangling a little, and spat out a sound, "Twee."

The table erupted into smiles and laughs.

"There is something there, after all," said Bear.

The boy looked intimidated by the sound and the expressions. The laughter and teeth-baring smiles were hard for him to interpret. It looked like aggression and challenges.

Oscar didn't notice the boy's withdrawal, "Did he say Twee? That's not a name. That's a sneeze."

He pantomimed a sneeze, "Ah... Ah... Ahhhh... Twee!"

Anne noticed that the boy looked intimidated. "It's alright, Twee. We're happy."

Bear tried an experiment, calling out the name quietly, and seeing if the boy responded. It seemed he did.

Anne had a sudden inspiration. "Twee," she said. "How old are you?"

The boy held up his right hand with two fingers raised.

Anne laughed with delight. "Maybe he was two when they lost him," she exclaimed.

# 3

Anne attempted to keep Twee behind closed doors for a few more days so he wouldn't run away. Soon, it became clear he was so attached to her that he wasn't going to. She provided him with food that was more plentiful and better than anything he had ever had. She provided him with a feeling of safety, and she offered him attention.

Twee followed Anne around the camp like a faithful dog. She reminded him of Ash, who helped raise him when he and the rest of the pups in his litter were still living in the den with Misha.

Some children ran around the camp like wild dogs, free-range children. They started following Anne and Twee, chanting, "Anne's got a puppy. Anne's got a puppy," until she threw things at them to chase them away.

The camp was large. Twee could not conceive of the number of creatures or animals who lived in it, so he tried not to think of it. When he got separated from it, his pack had seemed sizable to him. Whenever he saw more than one person coming, he tried to disappear into Anne's shadow.

Oscar and Bear kept track of Twee's progress. All three of them: Oscar, Bear, and Anne, were gratified when he displayed signs of normal behavior.

"What could have happened to him?" wondered Oscar. "We don't know anything about his life before we found him in that cell."

Anne tried to teach Twee to speak. He seemed totally without language, but his brain was reasonably developed, so he retained things and learned quickly. She began by just pointing at things and saying a word. He was much more interested in learning how to understand than he was learning how to speak.

Words that had something to do with food were a priority.

Twee got comfortable wearing trousers but couldn't deal with shoes or shirts. His hair had begun to grow back, so his head sported a little short stubble. He moved with a quick animal grace that made him look uncanny.

Initially, Anne had Twee sleeping on an extra cot in her room. She set him up in the tent next to hers once he got a little more comfortable living in the camp. After a while, he was relaxed enough that he began wandering around camp on his own. He still followed Anne whenever she went anywhere, but he occasionally went out by himself. In the beginning, his solo expeditions were usually to the mess tent.

Money wasn't used in the Raven's camp. There also wasn't anyone there who wasn't part of the band. There was an area (mostly just a tent over some benches and tables, with a stew pot simmering nearby) where people went to eat. The members of the Raven's band called it the mess tent. Someone was always tending the stew pot. Food was tight, but what they had was for the use of the Raven's people. Food would be available for you if you needed it, especially if the crew tending the stew pot recognized you.

Twee became a familiar sight in the mess tent. He had accepted many aspects of his new life. The amount and variety of food available to him still roiled his world.

"Hey, it's Anne's puppy," said someone by the pot.

"Anne's puppy is always hungry," said another voice as someone handed him a bowl of stew.

Twee took his bowl and went to sit at a table in the corner. The seats were a little big for him, but he made do. The stew in the bowl was the top priority.

Two young men sat at the other end of the table. Both looked tired.

"I had Bear for my drill instructor today," one said.

"That's harsh," said the other, "Try not to have him use you as a sparring partner. He really packs a wallop."

Twee focused on trying to understand what they were saying. It didn't really matter to him what these two people were talking about. Still, he wanted to learn to understand speech, and an overheard conversation was a chance to learn.

"So, they call him Bear because he's so big and strong and looks like a bear, right?"

"That's not what I heard."

"What other reason could it be?"

"Well, you know how they just built this fancy new outhouse building? They keep it clean and even try to clear out the roaches every so often?"

"What does that have to do with why everyone calls him Bear?"

"Well, I heard Bear won't use the outhouse. He refuses."

"I still don't get what that has to do with why they call him Bear."

"Haven't you heard the old line about where a bear goes to the bathroom?"

# 4

The Raven was an outlaw. The king's men wanted the Raven and all his crew for "high crimes and misdemeanors." He had started life as a simple gamekeeper. Several years back, under the reign of the current regent, when taxes started growing disproportionately, he took offense at how oppressed ordinary people were under the regent's rule. So he took up arms to defend the common folk. He stole from the rich and gave to the poor. He would mostly steal tax collection revenue from the king's tax collectors. He would distribute funds he didn't need to support his men among the poor.

So at least went the stories the outlaws told new recruits and each other. The king's men probably told different tales. It's also likely that the common folk told a third type of story.

It was undoubtedly accurate that taxes were high of late. It was also verifiable that the common folk chafed under them. Another truth was that the current regent had something to do with the increasing taxes.

In these tales, what might be questioned is how much of the money the Raven's men stole went to the poor. Another question could be whether the money they took always came from tax revenue coffers.

The stories from these sources had three things in common: the Raven and his cohorts were being successful in their endeavors. The king's men were getting increasingly frustrated and desperate to find them. And although the king's men might be reluctant to admit this, the Raven treated his crew well.

The Raven heard of an obscure notion back in the days when he frequented the king's court before he became an outlaw. He made a point of making his men (and the smaller number of women in the camp) follow this notion's rules. It was called chivalry.

As far as what the Raven expected from his men and the people in the camp, it meant that you were supposed to be kind to people and not kill, maim, or abuse anyone who didn't deserve it.

It was very hard for some people in the camp and especially hard for some new recruits. Folks who wound up joining an outlaw band were often not people one might associate with good behavior.

The people who joined with the Raven came from all walks of life. Although one thing they had in common was that if they weren't in conflict with the law before joining, they were after.

Bear had been a farmer. He lived on a small farm, working with his family to make a modest living. (Even then, he hadn't been very fond of outhouses).

When the tax collectors came, his elderly father argued with them about the taxation amount. He insisted they would leave them without enough to keep the farm going. Bear was forced to run when he retaliated after the tax collector's guard struck down his father.

His father recovered, and Bear sent his family money when he could.

Oscar was a hedgewitch. There were three kinds of magical people; the learned mages who studied at the Academy, the cunning folk, and hedgewitches. If you asked a mage or a cunning person, they would tell you there were only two kinds of magical people. The hedgewitches knew differently.

The Academy-trained mages were the elite of the magic

people. You might find one at a castle of a duke or count. The cunning folk took care of the commoners. Each little village or town had one to brew love potions or cure sick cows. The hedgewitches were usually on their own out in the wilds.

It wasn't clear why Oscar was with the Raven. There were no stories of him having gotten in trouble with the law, and it didn't seem the king's men knew who he was.

Anne was a miller's daughter from a modest town (so small, many called it a village) in the countryside, far from the forest where the outlaws roamed. She had met a man and followed him to the camp. Her relationship with him ended long ago, but her relationship with the outlaw crew remained. She had considered trying to go home, but the king's men knew her face, and returning to her village would endanger her family.

# 5

After Twee was with the camp for a while, he acquired a knife from somewhere. It wasn't clear where. It might have been from Oscar or perhaps Bear. Perhaps even from Jordan, who Twee had run into a few times since his arrival.

It certainly wasn't from Anne. She frowned when she saw it. She didn't say anything as it was common for people to carry weapons in camp. In fact, it was unusual not to have something. She frowned when she saw it, as Anne remembered a time when she lived in a place where people didn't carry weapons, and in fact, most people didn't really know how to use one.

Twee felt better with the knife on his belt. He had felt toothless without it.

Twee made some progress with speaking and understanding speech. He seemed to understand a lot of what Anne said to him. Especially anything about everyday things in camp. His vocabulary wasn't extensive yet, and he still refused to talk. Anne was convinced Twee could speak if he chose to. He was just choosing not to.

There was a pack of boys who roamed the camp. They came from various different sources. There were some camp followers, and one or two had children. Several were runaways. A few had come to camp with a parent.

It was just boys, no girls. They were partially feral. Jordan had been part of the pack until recently. Now, he had matured enough to go on missions with the men.

The pack noticed Twee. They became aware of him how a wolf pack would become aware of some other predator within its territory. They didn't bother him when he followed Anne, but they stalked him sometimes when she wasn't with him.

There were nine or ten of them. The largest, a boy of about twelve, liked to wear crow's feathers in his hair. The other boys called him the Crow. He encouraged the nickname, perhaps because they lived in the Raven's camp.

They hadn't challenged Twee directly, but he'd heard calls of "Anne's Puppy" and "Mute boy" directed at him several times when walking around the camp.

They didn't seem to want to confront him with other people from the camp around. Twee got the feeling their roughness and rebellion mainly were an act, and they were biding time until they got old enough to join the outlaws like Jordan.

Twee started roaming a little further afield. He didn't restrict his wandering to just following Anne and going to and from the mess tent anymore. He started exploring the forests around the camp. He went out during the day several times, but he also wandered at night. He hadn't gotten over the years he'd spent as a nocturnal creature. Sleeping during the day and waking up as the sun fell still felt comfortable for him.

Anne was a bit bothered by him not getting up in the mornings. She had no idea how much he was up at night. She worried that he was getting lazy.

One evening, Twee headed out of the camp just as the afternoon daylight turned to twilight. The pack caught up with him.

The camp was large and busy. It was nestled in a valley in the hills, heavily forested and difficult to approach unless you knew where you were going. The ridgelines on both sides of the valley made it easier to walk past rather than into it. It wasn't hidden exactly. It was simply more likely that someone walking through the forest would follow the ridgeline and never walk down into the camp.

There were rumors that Oscar, the hedgewitch, had cast a spell on the woods around the camp that encouraged this behavior and made it even harder to find the valley. Whether this was true was something Oscar didn't talk about, and people didn't feel comfortable asking him.

When people entered and left the encampment, they tried to avoid walking the same way twice whenever possible. They didn't want any established trails to lead to the camp through the forest. As a nocturnal predator and hunter, Twee appreciated this little touch.

Twee left the camp. Slipping as quietly as he could out of the underbrush into a small clearing, he saw them waiting for him. The Crow's pack was arrayed in front of him in a semi-circle.

He could have slipped back into the underbrush and made his way back to camp with his tail between his legs. Perhaps that's what they expected him to do.

Instead, Twee stepped out of the underbrush into the center of the clearing. Into the center of the pack's semi-circle. The Crow was in the middle of the arc of boys. Four on one side and five on the other. He straightened as Twee approached him and said, "Anne's puppy. Mute, dumb, and dumb. We're gonna teach you some respect, mute boy."

It wasn't clear what the pack was actually going to do. A lot of their behavior was posturing. The Raven turned away people who weren't willing to follow his code of "Chivalry." While these boys were too young to have been asked, most of them had parents or friends in the camp who had.

Twee stepped forward and stood up straight himself. He was smaller than the Crow, who was several years older. He bared his teeth in a wolfish snarl and began a low rumbling growl. In the quiet of the forest evening, the sound echoed off the trees and the underbrush. It filled the clearing with menace. He put his hand on the hilt of his tooth.

The Crow looked startled. "What you think you're gonna do, puppy-boy?" he said. He tried to figure out how this situation was getting out of his control so fast.

Twee darted forward with uncanny quickness. His tooth emerged from its sheath and glinted in the twilight in his hand. His rumbling growl turned into a full-throated howl.

The pack scattered. The boys vanished into the underbrush with lightning speed. It wasn't long before Twee was alone in the clearing. A lone crow feather lying on the ground was all that was left.

It's not clear if that was when people in the Raven's camp started calling Twee "the Wolf." It was definitely when "Anne's puppy" turned into "Anne's wolf" for the Crow's pack.

# 6

Twee started to speak. His brush with the Crow's pack had given him confidence. He started using his mouth for something other than eating. He shared his first words, of course, with Anne. The first time he said a word, she felt like a proud mother. His first word was 'stew.'

Twee sat at a table in the mess tent with Oscar. It was something Twee had wondered about for a while, but he finally had a way to get an answer. The feeling of being able to express himself verbally was a revelation to him.

"Oscar," Twee said, "Hair... Face... Why?" Twee had started to speak, and after spending months listening, his vocabulary was not tiny. However, sentence structure was still beyond him. Twee felt the frustration of not being able to express himself clearly. Still, it was nothing compared to not being able to express himself at all.

Oscar put his hand on his chin. He stroked his beard for a second. He shaved it into vertical strips, one strip below the sideburns on each side and one down the center underneath his nose and mouth. The patches of hair were quite long and grew down below his chin. In between the strips, his chin and neck were clean-shaven. Most of the men in the camp who grew beards did it because it was easier than shaving. With the way Oscar maintained his beard, he still had to shave.

"You're asking about my beard? Normally I wouldn't talk about that. Trade secrets, you know," he said with a wink.

"There are lots of things we hedgewitches know," he continued. "Things the cunning folk and even the mages don't know.

"You know what a hedgewitch is, right?" Oscar said.

"Someone who can do a little magic but hasn't ever been to that fancy school they have over on that lake."

He breathed a deep sigh. "Also, someone who the cunning folk hasn't taken into their confidences. We're more loners. We talk to each other sometimes, but not to the degree they do."

He winked again at Twee. "Don't tell Bear this, but the potion I gave him, which he used to melt through the iron bars of your cell? I bought it from a local village's cunning woman. I never was great at potions. I can make something which will make you burp uncontrollably for ten minutes, but not something like that."

"Anyway, about the beard," he continued. "There's a kind of magic called Capillus. It's a way to generate power. The mages think it's pure superstition, and the cunning folk are skeptical. We hedgewitches use it to strengthen our magic. You can carve patterns in living hair that give the bearer more magical power. It helps a little with every bit of magic you do."

He stroked his beard again. "This design is my own," he said proudly.

Twee looked confused. He hadn't understood everything Oscar had said. He understood quite a bit, though, and he liked the sound of Oscar's voice. He understood enough to ask. "Women?"

"Good point," said Oscar. "You've noticed women don't grow beards. Well, hedgewitch women use Capillus as well. In fact, I think they do it even more than the men do. It's just you don't see it."

"Why?" said Twee.

"Well," said Oscar, "We can talk about that when you're a little older."

# 7

Jordan approached Twee one day. He had heard about Twee's encounter with the Crow's pack and saw that Twee had taken to wearing a knife. Jordan fancied himself a bit of a knife fighter. He was still only fifteen and hadn't reached his full growth, but it was clear he would not be the tallest of men. Given his size and speed, using a knife was a good option.

There was regular weapons training for every able-bodied person in the outlaw camp. Frequent raids went out for supplies, robberies, and tax revenue procurement. Sometimes the crew of the missions was made up of volunteers. Other times they weren't. There was the possibility of a raid by the king's men at any time. Their chief protection was that the king's men didn't know where they were, but that could change. A single disgruntled person could cause them all a lot of trouble. Having everyone know how to fight made sense.

The regular training was in the use of more conventional weapons. Bows, spears, and swords. The knife fighters worked a bit on the side. The people who wanted to learn to fight with knives mostly took it upon themselves to teach each other.

Jordan and Twee went to a clearing just outside the camp. Twee was initially confused about what Jordan was asking him to do. The knife was a part of himself. He used it when he needed it. He didn't understand the idea of learning to use it better at first. But when Jordan had him hold his knife hand forward and showed him how easy it was for him to disarm Twee, he changed his mind.

The two of them started training several hours a day. They used short wooden sticks with carved handles. They singed the edges and tips in a fire, so they made a black charcoal mark when they hit. Twee was quick, and it interested Jordan to find he did some things right. At first, he thought someone had already trained Twee to use a knife. But then he remembered the primitive creature they had taken from the cell, and he didn't know who would have done that.

It also interested Jordan to find that some things Twee did wrong seemed to work. Something about how he moved with his knife like it was a part of him made it so his unconventional moves could surprise his opponent.

Jordan continued to practice with the older outlaws. He didn't let them know he and Twee were training in knife fighting. He thought they might tell him Twee was too young, and he didn't want to stop.

# 8

Several years passed. Twee grew. One might have said he was tall for his age, but no one knew how old he was. He was wiry, light for his size, but he developed visible muscle on his arms and legs. He still didn't wear shoes and preferred not to wear shirts.

Inevitably brown hair replaced the shaved head he had after his initial session with Anne. The brown that the wood of the walnut tree showed on a tabletop or kitchen table when you have polished it with love and care. After a while, Twee realized he was comfortable with his hair being almost shoulder length. Anne tolerated this as long as it was kept clean and deburred frequently.

In the beginning, Twee still sometimes stumbled when he spoke. Though he learned quickly, he didn't always understand things people who grew up in more conventional settings learned at a very young age.

Anne tried to tell him about her childhood at one point and encountered unexpected difficulties. She started by telling him she was a miller's daughter, and his response was, "What's a miller?"

Even once he could speak well enough, Twee didn't tell anyone about his life with the wolves. At first, he wasn't sure how to explain it, then after a while, it began to seem like a dream. He thought so differently now. It was hard to believe it had really happened.

He was tempted to tell Anne several times, but somehow he felt she might look at him like an animal, and he couldn't imagine anything worse than that.

He acquired the nickname 'the Wolf' anyway, though no one knew how appropriate it was.

The camp changed a bit during that time. Not in any fundamental way. It got a little bigger. New people arrived occasionally, and sometimes people left on missions and didn't come back. The new arrivals outnumbered the people not returning from missions.

The Crow aged out of his pack's leadership and began to go on missions with the outlaws. Twee had gained the other boys' respect, and they followed him when he wandered in the forest outside the camp. Some of them learned to move stealthily in the night and got used to the darkness. The Crow's pack became known as the Wolf pack.

Twee kept training with Jordan. He was getting good with his tooth. His native speed, combined with the techniques learned, made him a formidable knife fighter.

Jordan considered introducing Twee to the adult outlaws he trained with even though he was young. He thought it would be interesting to see Twee spar with some of them. He even thought he wouldn't mind seeing one or two of them taken down a peg.

Twee stopped following Anne wherever she went. He let her go about her business and went about his own. He stopped following her everywhere she went, but he never stopped wanting to.

# 9

Somehow, the Raven noticed Twee. He didn't notice him in the sense of seeing him, talking to him, or even meeting him. He noticed him in the sense of learning something about who Twee was, something about what Twee could do, and that Twee existed.

Bear sounded out Twee one evening about whether he would be willing to work as a scout on a mission. They called their outings "missions" because, while many other words could have been used, "mission" made them feel more like freedom fighters and less like thieves.

"I wouldn't have asked," said Bear, "except the Raven asked for you, personally."

They were sitting in Twee's room next to Anne's. Bear made sure Anne was out before approaching Twee. He would happily face down the entire king's guard before facing an angry Anne.

Bear had some misgivings about asking Twee to do this. He was very young and, in many ways, still innocent.

Bear found it hard to refuse the Raven anything. The Raven had taken him in when he was on the run from the king's men and provided him with the means to help his family.

"It's a straightforward mission," Bear said. "There's a tax collector who made the mistake of traveling along a fairly predictable route. We're pretty sure we know where he will be a few days from now."

"What we need from you is some scouting," Bear continued. "The plan is to position yourself somewhere where you can see the convoy passing, but obviously, they can't see you. Then signal us with some natural sound, so we know they're coming."

"Do you know how to defend yourself?" he said. "The idea is for you to never be seen, but the best-laid plans, of bears and ravens, as they say."

Twee pulled his tooth from his belt and spun it around in his hand. He'd been practicing a little twirl spin move Jordan had taught him. It didn't really have a purpose, but it looked good.

Bear looked skeptical. "Well, it'll have to do, I suppose. We'll have to figure out some way for you to signal the men to tell them when it's time to attack." He said. "Do you think you could make a sound like a wolf?"

# 10

Twee crouched in the underbrush on the edge of the cleared area beside the king's road. The official roads, especially the ones tax collectors traveled, were kept clear on both sides to a distance of ten feet. It was the last gasp of twilight before total darkness fell. This stretch of the king's road went through a forested area. The Raven and Bear had selected it as the best spot for an ambush.

Twee's job was simple. He was supposed to make sure the convoy was about the size expected and that there were no surprises. When he determined that, he was supposed to give a wolf call, which would tell the Raven's men, waiting up ahead down the road, that it was time to, and safe to, attack.

Bear assured him they weren't looking for a fight, really. They would fire a volley of warning arrows and make a friendly announcement suggesting surrender was the best option. The intelligent guards would immediately give them the tax coffers, and everyone would be happy. Twee wasn't sure exactly how pleased the tax collector and guards would be, but he wasn't about to argue with Bear.

The signal Twee was supposed to give was a wolf call. The Raven's band had an expert tracker who was called Holter. Holter was assigned the task of teaching Twee to be able to give a wolf call. The first time Holter gave the cry that he wanted Twee to learn, Twee had to admit it wasn't too bad. If you accepted that the wolf Holter was imitating howled with the accent of stupid.

Holter refused to admit the sounds Twee made were better than his. The first time Twee made a wolf howl, Holter got a confused look on his face and looked at Twee like something was wrong with him, but after that, he insisted Twee learn to make the sounds as he did. Eventually, Twee gave up and learned to howl in the accent of stupid.

The convoy passed by. Twee felt he needed to hold his breath. The night didn't make him nervous. He was happy to be working with the adult outlaws on a mission. Still, being this close to this many armed king's men did make him cautious.

Twee counted carefully. As the last man passed, the count was under the upper limit Bear had specified for him. Now he was supposed to wait a certain amount of time and then give the howl that meant go ahead. The wait time was so the convoy was the proper distance ahead of where he was, so they wouldn't detect him.

Twee waited the specified amount of time then gave the call, with the appropriate accent of stupid. He started to rise to creep forward to see the encounter. He wasn't supposed to, but he couldn't let this mission finish without knowing what had happened. Anyway, he might be able to help.

As Twee started to move forward through the undergrowth, he hesitated. *What was that sound*?

He stopped moving and checked to make sure he still wasn't visible from the road.

Another troop of the king's men came marching around the corner. They had their armor muffled with leather under the metal to reduce the noise. Twee froze. This wasn't part of what Bear had described.

They were marching fast down the road. It wasn't clear if the soldiers were trying to catch up with the tax convoy or were intentionally keeping behind it to trap possible thieves.

Twee had to do something. There wasn't time to get to a safe distance. He was still hidden in the underbrush. Maybe he could get away in time.

He rose, turned to run away from the road, and gave a full-throated wolf warning howl. Twee left off the accent of stupid. He figured Holter would understand.

As he started to run, he saw the soldier's reactions out of the corner of his eye. The nearest ones looked terrified. They thought there was a wolf pack right on top of them. One of the officers near the front of the convoy had more presence of mind. He reacted quickly and called out, "That's not a real wolf. It's too close. Catch up with the tax convoy!"

While he encouraged the bulk of his men to hurry down the road, he sent a few off into the woods.

"Find whoever made that howl!"

# 11

Twee scrambled through the underbrush. He could hear the king's men crashing through the bushes around him. The officer had sent several men after him, some on one side and some on the other. Twee thought his best chance would be to go straight ahead quickly.

He darted from one patch of cover to the next.

"There he is!" he heard one of the men call out.

They were big men dressed in heavy armor. Twee should have been able to slip away like a wolf in the night, but it was several years since he had lived in the wild. He was bigger and slower than he had been. At one point, he tried to dart into a gap between two shrubs and misjudged the width. He got entangled and slowed down by the branches.

One of the guards caught up to him and grabbed him by the seat of his britches. The thought flashed through Twee's mind. *It's these damn britches every time! I need to go back to wearing nothing.*

Twee struggled and tried to break free, but the king's man strengthened his grip.

Twee turned to face the guard as best he could with the man's grip on his pants and pulled his tooth from his belt. The guard reached out his other hand, which wasn't gripping the seat of Twee's pants, and grabbed both Twee's fist and the knife hilt. He squeezed with his chain-mail gloved hand, and Twee cried out in pain.

Another king's man arrived. "Don't hurt him too badly," he said. "The captain will want to see him intact."

The second man took Twee's tooth out of his crushed hand. Twee felt the sense of helplessness he always had when he didn't have a knife. He felt like crying for a moment, but he turned it into a growl and tried to bite the man holding him.

The king's man clouted him on the side of the head. The heavily gloved hand was like lead, and Twee saw stars.

The king's men made their way back to the road. It was getting dark, and one of them produced a torch from somewhere.

There had been four of them hunting for him. For a moment, Twee felt a surge of pride that it had taken four of them to catch him. Then it faded in the realization of having been caught.

The captain had gone on ahead to meet up with the rest of his men. The four men realized they were separate from the rest of their cohort and hurried down the road to catch up. There were probably still outlaws in the woods.

There was a bit of disorder when they reached the tax convoy. The main wagon was stopped in the road's center, a line of arrows stretching across the dirt before it. The king's men were milling around all over the place. There was a rustling in the underbrush and torchlight showing through the trees as they searched for the outlaws.

The man holding Twee walked up to the captain and said, "Here he is, captain; we got him." He griped Twee by the back of his belt and lifted him up to show him to the captain. The belt was tight around Twee's waist and squeezed the breath out of him.

The captain looked disappointed. "That's just a kid. He's not going to know anything useful.

"These animals," he continued, "It's just like them, to have a barefoot kid doing a job like this and then abandon him when things turn sour. Did you see how they scattered like a flock of birds when they saw how many we were? They think they're wolves, but they're just rabbits.

"Throw him in the merchandise wagon with the others. We'll sell them at Grisput."

# SERPENT

# 1

The "merchandise" wagon was a prison cart. It relieved Twee to see there was no one he knew in the cart. His emergency howl must have gotten to the outlaws in time. There were three men of varying ages already in there. The wagon was roofed, but the sides were iron bars, and there was a locked, barred door on one side. It looked like an animal cage. The cart contained nothing except a bit of straw on the bottom and a bucket in one corner.

Twee looked at the other men in the cart. They were silent and looked sullen. He found a place on the cart floor near the one who looked the least threatening. The man looked at Twee and made a shushing gesture with the whispered comment, "They hit us if we talk."

After sitting for a while, men coming and going, torchlight bouncing off the trees and off the cart, the convoy began moving. The wagon lurched into rumbling motion. There were two horses harnessed to the cart and a driver sitting in the front. Twee kept hoping something would happen as they traveled the night through the forest.

Twee kept hoping, but looking at the number of men marching both in front and behind the cart, he knew his hopes were vain. After a while, he hoped nothing would happen, as the feeling of strength from the marching cohort was overwhelming.

Still, his heart sank when the cart and the cohort rumbled out of the forest.

Twee checked his hand to see how bad it was. It hurt, but he didn't think anything was broken. They hadn't had regular schooling in the outlaw camp. Still, everyone was required to learn things that were necessary for survival. One of the skills they considered valuable was basic field medicine. Twee knew enough to believe his hand would recover.

Anne, of course, schooled Twee on the side. In addition to what she taught him about reading, writing, and arithmetic, he learned the basics of running a mill.

When the cart rumbled into the large town that was the convoy's first destination, Twee stared through the bars with his mouth open.

It was a walled town. The walls were beyond Twee's comprehension; they were so tall. And stone. Twee wouldn't have imagined there was that much stone in the world.

A crowd of people was queuing up to get past the king's men guarding the gate. The guards asked questions and sometimes refused entry or exit to people trying to pass through.

Twee was bewildered by the sheer number of people at the gate. He had thought the Raven's camp grand. The number of people waiting to enter this town made the encampment look tiny.

In addition to the crowds of people, there were countless animals. Every cart was pulled by mules or horses. Farmers were trying to get to market with their livestock. Chickens clucked, cows mooed, and donkeys and mules brayed.

At one point, a dog made its way past the cart. The hairs on the back of Twee's neck rose. He felt an instinctive growl of challenge start to rise from his belly. There weren't any dogs in the outlaw camp, and Twee hadn't encountered one before.

The convoy was waved on past the line. The uniform of the king's men and especially the cohort's captain was identification enough.

This city wasn't their final destination. The tax collector stayed when they left, but the cohort traveled on. Twee lost track of the number of towns, some bigger and some smaller, they passed through. Of course, he had no idea of their final destination.

His companions didn't totally refuse to speak to him. There were times when the guards weren't around or when it was dark when they could have whispered conversations. The three of them, and a fourth who joined them as they passed through one town, were townsfolk accused of crimes and thrown on the "king's justice."

The local government would decide guilt, innocence, and punishment in the smaller towns that didn't have a sheriff or judges. Sometimes the penance would be whipping, exile, or other things, but a frequent sentence was the "king's justice." This meant turning the accused criminal over to any of the king's men passing by.

The "king's justice" was mixed in its effectiveness. It depended a great deal on the officer in charge's temperament. It also varied based on his willingness to do paperwork.

The captain of this cohort was fond of a solution, sometimes referred to as the Grisput resolution. The Grisput resolution reduced paperwork and helped improve his temperament by providing him with an income.

Twee soon became quite familiar with the Grisput resolution.

## 2

The cohort marched into Grisput. Twee was more used to walled cities and city gates by this point, but he still watched the crowds with fascination. Grisput wasn't the largest city they had traveled through, but it had the most secure gates. And the highest and most secure-looking walls.

The city's flag flew over the walls and the guard checkpoints. The flag had a purple background, with a coiled serpent silhouetted in black in the center.

Unlike in many of the cities that the troop had traveled through on their way to Grisput, the guards at the gate weren't wearing the king's men's blue tabards with the black lion head silhouette. The Grisputian guards had their own uniforms. They had tabards in the same purple as the flags flying over the walls, and they had the same silhouetted coiled serpent on the front.

The guards at the gate were very thorough in their security checks. They turned more people away than at the entrances to other cities. Interestingly, they stopped people from leaving as much, if not more, than they prevented them from entering. They even checked the captain's papers. Something Twee hadn't seen before.

The walls of Grisput felt stronger, higher, and darker than the walls of other walled towns they had traveled through. Twee wondered if they were so high to keep people out or to keep people in.

As the cart rumbled through the city streets, Twee noticed something odd. The people the wagon was rolling past were a strange mix. Some looked elegant and nicely dressed, and others walked side by side with them, dressed more plainly and seeming needier.

The cart rumbled into a vast cobbled city square. A sizable

amphitheater took up one side of the space, teeming with people. The cobbles of the square led right up to the edge of the open auditorium. You could walk from the plaza and take a seat. You could hear the shouts in the amphitheater from the square. In fact, it was hard not to.

"Welcome to the slave markets of Grisput," said one of the other prisoners. He hadn't spoken to Twee before, and he didn't speak in a whisper.

One of the guards pounded on the bars of the cart with the butt end of his spear.

"Quiet in there," he shouted.

The scene in the square was one of chaos. The amphitheater's action felt distant, though the sounds were loud enough to reach every corner of the court. There were fewer animals here than there usually were among the crowds at the gate. Twee noticed a few dogs scavenging in the shadowy places under the eves of the buildings bordering the square. Even that far away, he felt his hackles rise.

It was like a market day or a festival. Twee had never experienced either of those things, so he found himself gazing around open-mouthed.

Vendors were selling various foodstuffs. A trendy thing to eat was "squirrel on a stick." Several vendors loudly expressed the opinion that this was a delicious thing that everyone should try. Some people in the crowd and some sitting in the amphitheater were here for the atmosphere. Others were very focused and were about urgent business.

Some children were running around the square as well. People regarded them in somewhat the same way as the dogs. They were mostly ignored, but they would be eyed with suspicion or sometimes struck if they got too close to someone. Some were the children of the more affluent visitors to the square, while others looked like street urchins.

Lying beside various booths selling things, there were bits of debris. More debris blew across the cobbles on the edges of the square: wrappings and other waste. The children and the dogs could sometimes be seen poking through the trash, trying to find valuables or food.

There was a crowd of people on one side of the square, surrounding a canvas-covered booth. Behind the tent were rows of iron-bared cages. The cages were filled with people. Sometimes only one to a pen, sometimes more. The men and women in the cells appeared to vary significantly in what they wore, how old they were, and many other things. Most of them had an impression of despair or hopelessness in common.

One cage, holding a large, burly-looking man dressed in animal skins, stood out from the rest. The man stood, his hands on the bars, shaking them, and howling with anger. His cries were loud but didn't rise above the square's general din unless you were close.

A crowd of spectators stood in a semi-circle in front of his cage, watching him and talking. Occasionally, trying to impress someone, one of the spectators went a little closer or baited the man. The crowd buzzed with pleasure when he responded with another roar.

The cart clattered over the cobbles into the square. People stepped quickly to the side to avoid the horses or, if they didn't step out of the way fast enough, stepped aside when the cart driver yelled at them or cracked his whip.

The captain and several of his men were still with the cart. The other guardsmen were attending to things elsewhere in the city.

The cart clattered up and stopped beside the booth in front of the cages. The captain stepped forward. Twee was close enough to hear what was said.

"I want to speak with the steward," said the captain.

A tall man stood inside the booth. Perched atop his head was a floppy black felt hat with a bright red feather drooping down from the back. He replied, "I can help you. What do you need?"

The captain turned to face him fully and repeated, "What

I need is to speak to the steward."

The man frowned, then disappeared through a flap in the back of the booth.

# 3

A voice boomed out, "Who calls for the Steward of the Bond market?" The steward stepped through the flap in the tent. He was a big man dressed in heavy green velvet robes. The steward wasn't big in the sense of being tall. He was big in how he seemed to fill the entire booth. A mountain of green velvet. He sounded annoyed when he first called out, but he broke into a smile after stepping into the tent and seeing the captain. You wouldn't have expected it for a man in his line of work, but the steward had a smile that lit up the room.

"Captain," he boomed heartily. "They didn't tell me it was you. Jonas is new."

He laughed a resounding laugh, walked over to the captain, and slapped his back.

"What do you have for me today?"

"I've got five," the captain said. "Varying ages and health." The captain didn't smile. In fact, the expression on his face got a little darker as the steward laughed. "They're in the cart over there. I'll leave the cart here and come and get it tomorrow."

"Terms?" said the steward. Then he smiled again and said, "Oh, that's right, you don't like paperwork. I'll have one of my men get as much information as is available from one of yours."

The steward winked at the captain and said, "Always happy to do business with our men in blue. Your usual extra credit, in addition to the payment?"

The captain scowled again and nodded curtly as he turned to leave.

Twee watched this transaction, and while he didn't understand all of it, he understood enough to be scared. As he watched the captain walk off, he felt an unexpected sense of abandonment. He hated the captain for taking him away from his life, but he was terrified of not knowing what was coming next.

The sun was setting over the building on the edge of the square. It was clear from the sounds coming from the amphitheater that the market was getting ready to close for the day.

Two burly men stepped over to the cart to unload the "merchandise." The last remaining king's man was in the booth talking to Jonas. The men opened the barred door and climbed in to grab one of Twee's companions. Twee thought for a second about trying to make a run for it, but the men were blocking the door, and he had no idea where he would, or could, go.

A smaller tent, a canvas roof covering a table and some chairs, was beside the booth. The burly men brought the prisoner over there, where they did something Twee couldn't see before putting him into one of the cages.

They came back to the cart then. It was Twee's turn.

The men brought Twee to the smaller tent and held him still while a third man, sitting at the table, raised a thin, unusually shaped curved knife. He reached out with the blade in one smooth, practiced motion and sliced a sizable chunk out of Twee's left earlobe. Twee flinched and realized why the men were holding him so tightly.

The man with the knife put it back down on the table, poured a drop of something from a small bottle he had sitting on the table onto the cut on Twee's ear, and folded a little white cloth pad into Twee's belt.

He did all of this in complete silence.

The two burly men dragged Twee out of the tent and roughly thrust him into one of the cages.

Twee fell to the ground, his ear burning. He felt like sobbing for a moment, then decided he couldn't give them the satisfaction.

"Hey, kid," came a quiet voice from the other side of the cage. "My name's Reynard. What's yours?"

# 4

Twee sat up. His ear burned, and he felt something dripping down his left cheek. "You've got some cherry juice on your cheek there, new-blood," Reynard said. "That's what the cloth they stuffed into your belt is for."

Twee pulled the white cloth from his belt and held it to his ear. The liquid the man had put on his ear made it sting. There might be more of that liquid on the cloth, as well.

He looked over at who was talking to him. Reynard was sitting cross-legged on the floor in the corner of the cage. He looked old to Twee. Twee guessed he might be about Oscar's age. Green eyes, a reddish shade to his hair, hinting at gray at the temples. He had a friendly smile on his face. Twee noticed Reynard was missing a chunk of his left earlobe as well. It didn't look recent. It was an old, healed wound. Reynard spoke quietly, like a man who knew how not to draw attention to himself.

"Are you new to Grisput or just new to the slave market?" said Reynard.

"Twee," said Twee.

"Chirp," said Reynard, "See, I can make bird sounds too."

"It's my name," said Twee, "You asked my name."

"Oh," said Reynard. "I guess I'll assume the answer to my question about how new you are is new to the entire world. With a name like that, you must have just gotten here.

"Anyway, Twee," Reynard continued. "Sometimes, when they're feeling particularly kind, they throw a new-blood like yourself in with an old hand like me. I guess they think I'll educate you or something.

"It doesn't always work," Reynard winked. "Sometimes, the vet eats the new-blood for lunch."

Reynard seemed to realize this comment hadn't been

taken quite the way he intended it to be from the stunned expression on Twee's face.

"I don't mean literately," he said quickly.

"So," Reynard went on. "I guess I'll assume you don't know anything about the Bond Market of Grisput. I'll start from there."

Twee nodded, but as Reynard talked, the sinking feeling in the pit of his stomach got worse. He hadn't thought he could fall any lower than being a prisoner of the king's men, but he had.

Reynard straightened up as he started speaking, and Twee wondered if he had been a teacher in another life. Or perhaps, he just liked to hear his own voice.

"Grisput is a city-state, like several of the cities in the kingdom of Liamec. They nominally owe allegiance to the king (or, right now, the young regent) but set and maintain most of their own laws.

"Indentured servitude is illegal in the more advanced cities of the kingdom. But, it's an essential piece of the economy of Grisput. Stop me if I'm going too fast." Reynard made this last comment with a smile.

Twee understood some of what Reynard said, but the last bit was too much for his vocabulary. "Indentured servitude?" he asked.

"Debt bondage. You owe some money, and your purchaser will make you work until you pay it off. You're an indentured servant or a bondsman. Hence the 'bond' market."

"But I don't owe anyone money," said Twee.

"The king's men take a shortcut," said Reynard. "I saw your friend, the captain, over there."

"He's not my friend," Twee said with a scowl.

"I know. I was kidding," said Reynard. "Anyway, the king's men, our boys in blue, if they catch a criminal, someone who's wanted in any major way, they bring them back to their headquarters. With people no one will miss, they sometimes use something they call the Grisput resolution. They sell them in Grisput. Make a pretty penny on the side."

"But I still don't owe anyone any money," Twee insisted.

"Course you do, kid," said Reynard. "They caught you doing something, set an arbitrary fine, decided you don't have the money to pay the fine, and that's what you owe. They won't tell you how much it is or how long it will take to pay it off. At some point, if you're lucky, years from now, someone will tell you your debt is paid. If you're lucky.

"Of course, they claim you're a free man or woman, no different from anyone else, once your debt is paid. Let me tell you, though, you'll never see anyone with a clipped ear living on High Street in Grisput. Or at the king's court."

Twee's face grew longer with each word.

"Sorry, kid," said Reynard. "Welcome to Grisput, or Grease pit, as some of us locals like to call it."

# 5

Twee woke in the night. The moon shone down on the bond square cobbles. Though there was a little straw on the cage floor, Twee felt colder than he ever had. The temperatures had been bitterly cold in the cart at night on the way here, but there were five people in a small space. He remembered back to the nights when he had been a wolf. Naked in the winter. How could he be colder now? He remembered cuddling next to Yip each night of his life as a wolf.

A tear rolled down Twee's cheek. He moved over closer to Reynard, who was snoring like an ox. Twee tried to borrow a little body warmth from Reynard and silently sobbed himself back to sleep.

Twee woke to the cage shaking as one of the burly men of the night before smacked the cage door bars with a wooden truncheon. Twee started thinking of the burly men as generic. They were burly-men, not individuals. It didn't seem like they were taking people out of the cages yet; they just wanted them awake. The burly-man walked down the row of cells, striking each door with his club.

Twee noticed the cage which had contained the wild-man yesterday was empty.

"Where's the guy who was doing all the yelling?" he asked Reynard.

Reynard laughed.

"I thought so," he said. "He was a plant."

"A plant?" said Twee, thinking he was reasonably sure the wild-man was a human being.

"An actor," said Reynard. "He was putting on a terrific show for the rubes yesterday. I bet they hired him to yell like that to entertain them and drum up business."

Twee frowned. Something was bothering him; he asked Reynard about it.

"Why are you here again, Reynard?" he said. "Haven't you already been sold?"

"Three times. They keep returning me. I'm not cooperative enough, they say. You don't want to see my back."

Reynard sighed. "I've got to be careful. Eventually, they may ship me off to the mines or something."

Twee's ear had scabbed over. It still hurt if he touched it, but it wasn't bleeding. There was a big chunk of the earlobe missing. He could see how it would be easy to recognize quickly if someone was a bondsman or not.

Several of the burly-men came back. They grabbed one side of the first of the cages in the row with a person in it and tilted it up at an angle. The man inside wasn't expecting this, and he lurched and fell. The burly-men ignored him. The bottom of the steel-framed enclosure had wheels on it, but the wheels fit into holes in the cobblestones, so it didn't move when the cage was in place. Once they tilted it up, Twee could see a track running under the pen, which the wheels fit into. They rolled the enclosure off in the direction of the amphitheater. More men were waiting with another empty pen, which they rolled into place to replace the one leaving.

They repeated this with the following cages. Soon, it was Twee and Reynard's turn. The pen rolled along the track behind the booths and the amphitheater. Twee could see the square was mostly empty. It was still early morning. The morning fog was clearing. Most of the people here were setting up booths for the day or working for the bond market.

The cage rolled along the track through an entrance behind the amphitheater and a stage. It joined with the rest of the enclosures brought from the receiving area.

Twee looked over the rest of the cages and the people inside. Most of them were shivering in the morning air. There were people with freshly scarred ears and whose scars had healed, but each had the distinctive cut earlobe that he carried.

Reynard looked resigned and just seemed to bide his time. There was nothing to do but wait.

The bond market square started filling with people. It was a festive atmosphere again, like yesterday. The people in the plaza seemed happy to be there, except for the ones in the cages.

There was bustling in the bond market area too. Twee and Reynard could see parts of both the backstage area and the stage from where they were situated.

"I'm not sure what advice to give you, kid," said Reynard. "I may know a lot about how this works, but I'm not good at solving it.

"What I do," he continued, "is try not to give them the satisfaction of knowing they have me beat.

"Though," he went on, "they have." For the first time since Twee met him, Reynard lost his smile.

The crowd started filling the seats in the amphitheater. People began gathering on the stage as well. Several burly-men surrounded another man on the stage. The burly-men were very deferential to him. He was dressed in the same purple as the Grisput flag background and had a sizable bright gold medallion on his chest. It might be a badge of office.

The bustling increased as everyone behind the scenes began getting ready for something. Then the steward stepped onto the stage as the man with the medallion called out in a piercing voice. "The steward of the bond market will now open the market!"

The steward stepped up onto the boards. He looked even more immense in the blazing morning sunlight than in the booth the night before. He was a bright green mountain moving onto the stage.

The steward lifted a little hammer and struck a gong that the burly-men had set up. The solemn sound rang throughout the amphitheater and the square.

"I declare the Grisput bond market open!" the steward announced.

A moment later, he continued, "And yield to the auctioneer."

The steward stepped off the stage, and the man with the medallion stepped forward.

The auction began. After the initial introduction of each merchandise piece, the auctioneer started the bidding and proceeded to rattle out numbers and respond to bids from the crowd at a mind-boggling pace. In some sense, the bidder wasn't buying a person but rather a bond contract for the person's time, but the effect was the same.

Soon enough, they were coming for Twee. Reynard, who complained about being left for the bargain bin at the end, was still there. As the guards approached the cage, he leaned his face into Twee's and said in a low voice, "Good luck, lad. Keep your head down and take care of yourself."

Two burly-men grabbed Twee's arms and pulled him toward the block.

# 6

The block was a literal block. It was a chunk of wood about a foot high and approximately four feet square. A notch was carved into the back that formed a step deep enough for a person's foot. Among the bond market's callousness and cruelties, providing this step so the merchandise wouldn't have to step too high to get onto the block seemed unexpected.

The weight of many feet, most of them bare, had worn the block down. In a different context, the worn wood could have seemed beautiful. The oils and sweat had softened the wood until it glowed a deep brown, stippled with black in spots.

The block's purpose was to raise the merchandise higher so that the people in the furthest amphitheater seats could see it and center it so that it was the stage's focus.

What happened next was a blur to Twee. He had never seen so many people in one place before, and they were all staring at him. He couldn't focus on what the auctioneer was saying, and he said a lot of it so fast Twee might not have been able to follow it if he had.

It seemed his youth and health were being used as a selling point. Twee didn't even know how the money system worked. They hadn't used money much in the outlaw camp, and Grisput had its own currency as an independent city-state. So he had no idea what was happening during the bidding.

The burly-men dragged him off the block a little later. They took him to a staging area, where he was given a lecture on obedience and inspected for cleanliness. It struck him that they hadn't focused on discipline. What if he didn't listen to his "owners" and ran away the minute he was out of the bond square?

Twee realized the city itself was part of what imposed discipline. He remembered the guards at the gate and how they turned away people trying to exit the city. There was no way someone with a clipped ear could leave without an excellent reason.

They also secured a set of lightweight shackles on him. They attached thin metal bands connected by a woven metal cable to his hands and feet. They allowed him to move a bit but restricted freedom of movement enough that certain things would be difficult, like running or wielding a weapon. There were keyholes in the bands around his ankles and wrists.

The burly-men dragged him out of the staging area and into another section where he could see people who looked like customers. There was a small group of people waiting for them. Jonas stood there, talking to three others. As the burly-men dragged Twee up to the group, he could hear Jonas finishing a practiced speech.

"... as we were saying, this is an 'As Is' sale. There wasn't any training done, so you'll be responsible for that yourself. The shackles are the Bond Market's property, so if and/or when you don't need them anymore, we'll expect them to be returned. Of course, if you have any problems, please come to us first. We have trainers, disciplinarians, and other experts on call who will be glad to help with any issues you might have."

The three people standing in front of Jonas listening to his patter were a family unit. Mother, father, and son. The father was a big man. Not in the sense that the steward was big but tall and muscular looking. He wore a faded red dyed linen tunic, stretching a little to accommodate his shoulders and biceps.

The mother was almost as tall as her husband. She wore a high hat that towered over both of them. Twee had noticed the headgear of the people in the bond square in the back of his mind. The men usually wore simple linen caps. The women (the free women, not the bondswomen) were trying to eclipse each other with their hats.

Not all the hats tried to outdo each other with height. Some were brightly colored, some were wide, and some were outrageously feathered. While Jonas talked, the mother was paying only half attention. The rest of her attention was focused on the hat of whatever woman walked by.

Her hat was a towering edifice of silk and velvet. It surprised Twee that she could hold her head upright. There were patterns in red, blue, and green in the fabric, stretching to the peak. Trailing in the wind from the very top was a lace veil.

The son, in contrast to his parents, seemed small. He was probably a couple of years older than Twee and a little taller. But, standing between his wide father and his extravagantly be-hatted mother, he looked diminutive. He was trying to sneer at what Jonas said, but he wasn't very good at it.

Jonas wound down his spiel. He turned to see Twee being pulled up to the group and said, "Ah. Here we are."

The big man looked skeptical for a second.

"He looks smaller than he did up on stage."

Jonas quickly reassured him, "He may be a little small, but he's healthy as a horse. Of course, we check their teeth as well. He should be able to do what you need."

The mother looked at Twee and said, "Do you speak? What's your name, boy?" She looked skeptical, as well.

Twee looked down at the ground. Wearing the shackles made him feel small and helpless. "Twee," he said.

Worried something might be going wrong with the sale, Jonas hurriedly handed the man some keys. "Here are your keys," he said. "Enjoy your purchase," he called out over his shoulder as he hurried off.

"Twee?" said the woman. "Nonsense. We'll call you David."

# 7

They walked through the city streets for a while, then Twee was ushered into a dark little room in a house. The family walked in relative silence. Twee wasn't sure what to say or what was his place to say. The son complained most of the way about his feet hurting. As soon as they left the bond square, the mother removed her hat and carried it carefully in her hands.

The father showed Twee into the little room and patted him on the shoulder as he shut the door. As the door was closing, Twee heard the mother call out, "We'll let you know your duties in just a bit, David."

Twee looked around the tiny room. A cot on one side took up most of the room's space. A little end table with a single drawer took up a lot of the rest. The limited amount of light and air coming into the room filtered through a high open window. The window was too high for Twee to look out unless he stood on the cot. There was a wooden shutter on the outside, which was partially closed.

Twee climbed up on the cot and peered out the small window. There was a busy city street outside. People, animals, and carts of various kinds were going by in both directions. Smells wafted in the window as well. Twee had smelled the cities the king's men brought him through on his way here. Mostly in passing, and the smell of the cart overpowered a lot of the city smell. He felt a moment of panic as he realized he would probably be smelling this smell for a long time.

Twee climbed down and sat on the cot. He inspected his chains and the bands on his wrists and ankles. There was a small hinged compartment on one of the wristbands with a label inside. It was an identification tag. It identified who owned him, or at least who owned his bond.

The bands and cables were designed to be worn full time or, at least, have the option to be. They were light enough that they could be slept in if need be. Twee hoped there wouldn't be a need.

Later, Twee was brought out into the central common room and sat down on one side of a wooden table. The father of the family sat opposite him. The mother hovered nearby for a moment, then went into the next room. Twee got the impression she felt talking to Twee should be the father's job, but she wasn't sure she trusted him with it.

"Now, son," he said. "Twee, is it?"

"David," came a voice from the next room.

"David," said the man reluctantly. "Let me tell you, David," he continued. "I didn't grow up in Grisput. I don't know what I think about this bondsman stuff. I've lived and worked here for quite a few years. Everyone swears the system works well, and it's necessary to maintain the state, but I've gotta tell you I'm not sure I like it."

"Thor!" came a cry from the other room.

The big man stopped and said to Twee, "Just a second, wait right here. I'll be back."

He stood and went into the other room. As the door shut, Twee heard him say something indistinctly.

The next words from the other room were loud enough that Twee could hear them through the closed door.

"That's not the way you talk to a bondsman! You tell them what to do! You don't ask them!"

The voices got quieter again, and Twee couldn't follow what was said.

The big man came back into the room. He shut the door to the room behind him as he walked in. He looked a little embarrassed.

"Sorry you had to hear that, son," he said. "Just a little difference of opinion. I guess we skipped a step. Introductions.

You, I know, are Twee. I'm Thor. My wife's name is Maria, and my son is Baldur."

"Anyway," he continued, "I'm a blacksmith. Have been my whole life. My father was a blacksmith, and he taught me. I'm proud to be one and hoped my son would be too."

Thor frowned. "He's not. He worked reluctantly with me in the forge for the last few years, but he hates it, and truth to tell, he's shite."

"His mother says it's beneath him. I told her if it's beneath him, what does that make me? Anyway, the difference of opinion is whether I need an apprentice or a servant. Either way, I need someone to help me with the forge."

# 8

Maria showed Twee how she wanted him to clean the kitchen floor. Although Thor had said they bought his bond to help in the smithy, a bondsman needed to do what they were told. Twee hadn't even seen the forge yet. In the early morning, Maria came into the room they had left him in and told him to follow her.

They hadn't removed his chains, wrist, and ankle bands. Maria was insistent that one didn't do that so quickly. "A bondy needs to earn their family's trust. It isn't just given." Maria was fond of quoting sayings like that. Especially on this subject.

Twee knelt on the floor and scrubbed at a spot Maria insisted needed extra attention. He asked her, "Ma'am, Thor said your name was Maria. How do you want me to address you?"

Maria frowned.

"Mrs. Wodenswold would be proper," she said. "I suppose Ma'am is acceptable. Calling my husband Thor sounds inappropriate to me, but I suppose that's up to him."

As she was speaking, several emotions flashed across her face. As she said the name Mrs. Wodenswold, she looked momentarily unhappy. When she mentioned how he referred to her husband, the frown returned. That expression was often on her face when speaking about her husband.

Twee wondered why saying the name Mrs. Wodenswold made her unhappy. Maria Wodenswold sounded like a nice name to him.

After Maria finished her kitchen scrubbing lesson, she brought Twee to the forge. The forge was adjacent and connected to their home.

The Wodenswold's home and the forge were part of a

row of attached houses on a busy city street in the craftsman's district of Grisput. To one side was a cobbler and on the other a wheelwright. Twee had stood on his bed to watch people rise and go about their business on the street in the early morning. It fascinated him. He had never seen so many people living in such close proximity before. The smells enthralled him less. When he lifted his face to the high open window, the scents horrified and amazed him again.

While he looked out the window, Twee thought about whether he could climb through it. It might have been possible, though his chains would have made it difficult. The bigger problem, he realized, was what he would do once he was outside. No one in this city would help him. Between the chains and his clipped ear, he would be instantly recognizable.

Maria brought Twee to the forge. A door in the kitchen's back wall opened into Thor's smithy. She opened the door, pushed Twee through it, and then closed it again. She was either reluctant to enter the smithy or simply had no desire to.

Twee stood on the threshold of the smithy for a moment, wondering what he should do next.

The interior of the smithy was a big open room. Columns supported the high ceiling. All the internal walls had been opened up, and a vast cavernous space was left. Big wooden shutters were propped up above large open windows in the front wall facing the street and the back wall facing the buildings behind the smithy. The rear windows opened onto a small, rather dingy-looking stone-cobbled alley. Through the windows facing the street, the city life Twee had glimpsed in the morning rumbled by. Carts, wagons, street hawkers, urchins, and stray dogs. Everything passed by these windows.

There was a blast of warmth coming from what must be the forge itself off to one side of the space. A breeze blowing through the open windows helped, but the heat was intense. There were anvils, barrels of various things, stacks of firewood, bins of charcoal, and racks of tools scattered throughout the room. It was too much to take in, and Twee felt overwhelmed.

Thor spotted him from where he stood by an anvil. He was holding a massive hammer and wearing a smith's apron.

"Twee!" he called out.

"David!" came a voice through the door into the kitchen.

# 9

Twee learned to help in the forge. He hauled water and charcoal, shoveled the charcoal into the forge, and manned the bellows. His morning started with sweeping out the smithy, even before the family sat down to breakfast.

Maria reluctantly agreed that Twee could sit at the table with the family for meals. She didn't entirely approve, but it was easier than giving him something to eat separately.

She had yellow-dyed linen placemats, which she set out on the table before each meal. She kept a separate rough woven burlap one for Twee.

She kept coming up with sayings from her childhood whenever one seemed relevant. Twee suspected they only heard the more polite ones. The one she remembered when they had the discussion about meals was, "A bondy is not family."

Twee began to enjoy helping in the smithy. It was hard work, and mostly, at this point, grunt work, but something about it was very freeing. He grew to appreciate the heat and exertion of working near the forge.

Twee found it exciting when Thor wielded his hammer, forging the heated iron. Twee would operate the bellows or shovel charcoal. The ringing of the hammer and the flying sparks, the forge's heat, and the sight of the iron being reshaped on the anvil made him feel part of something valuable.

Baldur ignored Twee. When he walked by him in the house, he would look away. At first, Twee thought Baldur didn't like him, but then he started thinking that Baldur didn't care about him exactly. He just didn't want Twee to exist. It wasn't that he was jealous of Twee working in the forge with his father. As far as Twee could tell, Baldur was happy about that. It was more like his world was simpler, and he liked it better if he could pretend Twee wasn't in it.

It seemed Maria felt the same way, except when she wanted Twee to do something for her. When Maria had Twee work on chores around the house, she tried to do it when Thor wasn't around. They seemed to have a debate or disagreement about whether Twee's time was only for the forge or for the household also.

Maria insisted Twee keep his chains on initially while he was with them. Thor acted as if he accepted this. But when Twee stepped into the smithy that first morning, as soon as the door to the kitchen closed, Thor pulled keys from his pocket, unlocked the chains, and removed them. "You can't wear those in here," he said with a wink. "It'd be dangerous." However, he put them back on Twee when they went into the house.

Thor and Twee ate breakfast and dinner with the family, but they handled lunch differently. Maria would give Thor something for lunch as he walked through the kitchen door into the smithy. It was just a door threshold away, but it was like Thor and Twee were going to a different world when they walked to the forge. They would spend the day there and only return to the house in the evening. Thor would sometimes forget to eat lunch, but unless Thor needed him, Twee would eat. He remembered being hungry from his life as a wolf and didn't like it. He took to opening the door to the dingy alley behind the smithy and sitting on the threshold as he ate.

After a few weeks passed, even Maria had to admit Twee was a model bondy. They removed the chains and put them into a closet somewhere. Thor reminded Maria they were supposed to return them to the bond market, but she replied it wasn't time.

Maria even agreed to allow Thor to show David around the craftsman's district to learn to run errands for the family.

# 10

The craftsman's district was close to the main gate into Grisput. As Thor showed Twee around during the next few days, he began to get a feel for the town's layout. Grisput was almost two cities. There were the lower city and the upper city. The two were separated by a high cliff, broken up with some narrow winding lanes, steep pedestrian stairways, and one wide switch-backed road called the Highway. Those who lived below sometimes referred to the Highway as the Highway to Heaven.

The craftsman's district, the bond market, some poorer residential districts, and the slums were in the lower part of the city. The upper part contained the governor's palace, noble residences, and the wealthier residential neighborhoods. High Street ran through the upper city and connected its districts.

Once Twee got out of the house and started following Thor around the craftsman's district, he could look up and see the cliffs and, on top of them, the homes and mansions of the upper city.

The craftsman's district was the wealthiest of the lower Grisput neighborhoods. It was filled with people who made things and solved problems for the rest of Grisput's citizens. As such, there were frequent visitors from the upper city wandering the district's streets. One of Maria's favorite pastimes was sitting by the window that faced the street in her kitchen and watching who walked by.

Twee heard her sometimes when he was sent in from the forge to get something for Thor (Thor didn't like coming back into the house until his workday was done), quietly saying things to herself like, "Oh. The marquis of Beiter." Or "is that the envoy's son?"

Of course, people and representatives from above the cliff attended the bond market also. Many of the be-hatted women in the bond market square were from upper Grisput, down in the market, to select a new bondy personally. Others were women from lower Grisput hoping to catch the eye of someone from the upper city and be thought respectable or just hoping to outdo the other women from the lower city.

Maria's pride was that she wasn't born and raised in the lower city. She also wasn't from upper Grisput. A small community of houses was halfway up the cliff between the two cities. The neighborhood was called Mezdor. It was a tight-knit group of families who tried to support and stand up for each other, as long as helping your neighbor didn't hurt your own standing. Those raised in Mezdor who cared about status felt superior to the lower Grisputians and longed to be upper Grisputians.

When Thor and Twee got near the main gate, they stopped and watched the crowds entering and exiting the city.

Twee and Thor stood on a higher area off to one side of the Main Gate Plaza. Being above the square and off to one side gave them a view of the action below. From their vantage point, they could see the crowds lining up below them, the cliff towering above on one side, and the high, dark city wall on the other. The main gate was next to the cliff's base. Upper Grisput was invisible from here, high above the cliff face.

The milling crowds and the hustle and bustle of people and animals fascinated Twee. Lines of people, carts, and livestock queued up to enter and exit. The guards screened people with great care. As Twee had noticed before, they applied extra scrutiny to people leaving the city.

Twee paid special attention when people who had the clipped ear that marked a bondy or wore chains approached the exit gate. At those moments, the guards became especially attentive. While Twee watched, they didn't allow anyone with a clipped ear out.

# FOX

# 1

Twee settled into his new life. Working with Thor in the forge was both a trial and a pleasure. It was hard work. He spent his days hauling wood, charcoal, water, bars of iron weighing half as much as he did, and pumping a bellows big enough that he had to jump to reach the handle to start.

But there was a pleasure in the creation of things. Twee didn't get to touch a hammer or even use a chisel to cut through a raw iron bar, but he got to see the beauty in Thor's smithing, and Thor was generous in his praise when Twee did things right. He wasn't cruel when things went wrong, but Twee could feel his disapproval. He was a hard man to disappoint.

When Thor didn't need him for a few minutes in the middle of the day, Twee would eat lunch on the back door stoop. The alley behind the shop was quiet. He was far enough from the forge, so the heat was just a glow of warmth on his back as he sat there in the open doorway.

Sometimes someone would pass by as he sat there, but the alley traffic was light compared to the main street traffic.

While Twee ate his lunch one day, a street urchin came down the alley. Twee was hungry and had barely taken a bite of his bread and cheese. In addition to the dawn sweeping, he had been manning the bellows for Thor all morning. He was tired and sweaty. His stomach felt like it wasn't a stomach so much as it was a hole in his belly where a stomach should be.

Twee sighed, broke his bread in half, and ripped off half of the cheese slice. As the urchin walked by, he held out the half sandwich. The urchin came over to him, hesitantly, as if fearing a trap.

It was a boy. Just a little shorter than Twee. Twee sniffed the air. On second thought, it was a girl. Her hair was cropped short, tangled like the knots in a fisherman's net, smeared with soot and dirt, but it might have been red underneath all that.

She wore a dirty burlap smock that stretched from her neck to her shins. There were no sleeves, just armholes. Interestingly, even though there were no sleeves, the dress was covered with pockets. They were sewn on by someone who didn't know how to sew but cared that they were secure and without holes. So they were slightly incompetently over-sewn.

Dirt and soot smeared her face, but her green eyes seemed intelligent. The way her eyelashes turned up at the corners was intriguing.

"I'm Twee," he said as she looked suspiciously at the bread. "What's your name?"

He thought perhaps she would take the bread and dart off without responding, but before accepting the food, she met his gaze briefly and said, "Vix."

She grabbed the bread then and took an eager bite. Twee initially felt he would miss the food later in the day, but when he saw how ravenously she devoured what he gave her, he didn't begrudge it. He took a bite of his own half.

They ate together. Vix stayed standing, peering around herself like she was suspicious that a group of the king's men would come running down the alley searching for her at any moment. Twee sat quietly on his stoop. They had in common how much they enjoyed their bread and cheese.

As they both finished, Vix looked Twee quietly in the eye again, gave him a shy smile, and whispered, "Thank you." Then she moved off down the alley. After she went a few steps, she drifted closer to the wooden wall that backed the other side of the lane and almost disappeared. The street urchins of Grisput weren't invisible. Still, they might as well have been, considering the amount of attention the city's citizens gave them. They faded into the background if they weren't directly in the way.

Later that evening, after Twee finished sweeping the kitchen floor, he walked past Thor and Maria's bedroom door as he went to his own room. He heard noises from behind their door and stopped for a second. He heard Maria's voice as she called out in a strange tone, "Oh, my barbarian!"

Twee was a little puzzled by this as he walked on, as based on his behavior, he didn't think of Thor as a barbarian.

## 2

The city-state of Grisput required certain things of bondholders. One of these was a tax. It wasn't a financial tax, though there were those also, but a time tax. The bondholder for a bondsman or woman in Grisput had to donate a small amount of that bond person's time annually to the city.

There was a Grisput holiday which took place in early May. Labor Day. Each year, on that day, city officials would take crews of bondys and compel their labor in various city projects.

Thor had a certain amount of leeway in deciding what job the city could use Twee's time for, but not about whether he would have to go.

"Lumber / Forestry," Thor read off a list posted on a bulletin board. "How's that sound, son?"

It sounded all right to Twee. He hadn't seen a tree, aside from little parks and things planted at the side of streets, since he'd gotten to Grisput.

The lumber crew approached the main gate. The bondys were chained together in groups of three. The coldness with which Twee and his fellow bondsmen were processed reminded Twee of his situation's realities.

The guards explained that the chains connecting each group of three bondys together were enchanted with tracking magic. Even if they managed to run, the guards would be able to find them.

The guardsmen started queuing up the bondys in their groups of three in the shadows of the cliff that rose to the upper city. Twee shivered, both with the morning cold and with excitement at the idea of seeing the world outside Grisput.

The guards marched the bondys out through the gates.

Twee was initially disappointed with what they could see on the other side. Low ramshackle wooden buildings blocked their view. The area immediately outside the gates was an even worse slum than the slum district back in the city. Some people the guards hadn't let into Grisput had made their homes here.

They marched through the outer slum and into open fields beyond. A staging area was set up further on, with guards waiting, flags flying, and rows of carts. The flags were the purple flag with the silhouetted coiled serpent that represented Grisput.

The bondys were loaded into carts. Then came a half-hour cart ride up into the hills above the city. As the cart carrying Twee and his chain-mates climbed the steep roads up into the heights, he took in the views and breathed the fresh mountain air deeply.

Twee was chained at the end of a threesome with two men. Both were older and larger than himself. Neither was in any mood for talking.

The cart lurched into a forestry base camp. There were crowds of men and guards here doing things that Twee didn't understand. He and the other bondys were kept waiting until they were assigned a task. Among the guards were men who were obviously loggers. Some guards were heavily armed, including a number with crossbows. Twee wasn't sure if the weapons were for if the group was attacked or if the bondys caused trouble.

Even where the bondys were kept, the view from the heights was spectacular. In the valley below, the walls of Grisput glowed in the late morning sun. There were fields all around lower Grisput and forest surrounding the heights of the upper city. You couldn't see the bond market, the slums by the gates, or the matching slum neighborhood within the walls from this vantage point.

Twee and the others in his chain-mate trio were assigned a new driver and cart. They were to go even higher into the hills. The driver was checking out an infrequently used logging road to see if it was clear and if there were sites where a logging crew should be sent. The bondys were along for labor if the road was blocked and needed clearing. No one bothered to explain this to them. They needed to overhear it and figure it out for themselves.

As the cart lurched and jerked along the rutted old logging road that led through the forest, Twee kept breathing in the mountain air. He had to fill his lungs. To fill himself with this air for when it was time to go back to the city.

Twee and his chain-mates sat on the back of the cart. They couldn't see the driver. Every time the wagon lurched or jerked, they would grab onto something for support.

The cart crested a slight rise and drove level. The bondys perched on the back relaxed just a bit.

The cart-horse gave a loud whinny, and there was the largest lurch there had been so far. Twee managed to get a grip on the side of the cart, but one of the three bondys slipped off. The falling bondy dropped to the ground behind the cart with a thud. There was a crunching sound. Twee thought the fallen man's leg must have collided with or slid under the wagon wheel.

The middle bondy briefly managed to maintain his grip on the cart. But the chain inevitably pulled him, and then Twee, off the wagon.

With a thud, Twee hit the ground. He felt the dull pain of the impact and heard the moans of the injured bondy. But what occupied Twee's attention first was the speed with which the cart rattled off down the rutted logging road.

Twee looked after the departing cart. It didn't seem to be slowing at all. He tried to stand up, then looked around himself to the sides of the road for the first time.

It became clear why the horse whinnied, why the cart was still speeding off, and why the cart driver hadn't stopped. Even if the driver had noticed the bondys falling off the wagon, he might not have stopped.

Standing on the side of the road, gazing curiously at the

three bondys lying in the logging road wheel ruts, was a wolf pack.

# 3

The lead wolf was bigger than the ones behind him. Twee was sure he was the alpha male, the father of this family. There were five or six wolves in the group. The whole pack looked at the bondys lying in the road, wondering what would happen next.

The bondy in the middle, who seemed uninjured, rose to his feet. Twee was between him and the pack. He started trying to move away from the wolves, but as soon as the chains binding him tightened on the man on the ground, he let out an even louder moan. Several of the wolves perked up their ears at the sound.

Twee felt overcome with a surge of elation. He remembered who he was. Over the years, he had lost his belief in his memories. He had never talked to anyone about his time with the wolves. He had almost come to think it never happened. But now, in this situation, he remembered, he believed.

Twee moved forward toward the lead wolf as far as the chain would allow. He leaned over and put his hands on the ground. He lifted his hindquarters into the air as high as possible and spread his legs and arms wide. He tilted his head to one side, exposing his throat, and made a throaty, whimpering sound, trying to sound pathetic and submissive. If he'd had a tail, he would have wagged it, but the best he could do was shake his butt around a little.

The bondy that wasn't lying on the ground moaning looked at him like he couldn't believe his eyes. The lead wolf tilted his head to one side. He made an uncertain, nickering sound. It was a sound Twee hadn't heard a wolf make before.

The lead wolf barked. Also, a sound Twee hadn't heard from wolves often. He likewise stepped forward, lowered the front of his body toward the ground, and spread his front paws wide to both sides. His tail started wagging like a metronome.

He bounced forward, raced up to Twee, and licked his face. Twee was startled. He hadn't been expecting this much success. In fact, he hadn't really been expecting success at all.

Twee got a whiff of a familiar scent. At first, he couldn't place it, then he remembered his first night in Grisput.

It was Yip. Somehow. From somewhere so far away, it was Yip.

Twee buried his face in Yip's neck fur. Yip smelled like home.

Twee looked into Yip's face. He looked older. His muzzle was a little gray and grizzled, he might have been through some hard times, but it was him.

Twee rose to his feet with one hand on Yip's back. The uninjured bondy stood as far from Twee as the chains would allow, staring at what was happening open-mouthed. The rest of the wolves in Yip's pack showed wolf versions of the same expression.

Twee looked at the pack and didn't recognize anyone. He wondered how this was possible. Yip must have dispersed from Sasha's pack, become a lone wolf, and wandered far from home before meeting a solo female and starting his own family.

Twee realized these wolves were relatives. His nieces and nephews. He knew there was no way they would understand any of this, so he maintained his distance.

Yip whined a happy whine and jumped up on Twee, putting his fore-paws on Twee's chest. Twee grabbed him in a hug, and they wrestled for a bit.

Twee felt happier than he had in years. He'd had pleasant moments in the outlaw camp and was starting to enjoy working with Thor in the forge. But, just now, he was back in the most joyful times of his childhood, playing with the other pups outside Misha's den.

The sound of a rumbling cart shattered the moment. Either the driver had somehow contacted the other guards, or it was him returning. It didn't matter which. Twee remembered the crossbows the guards at the lumber camp had and the one he had seen sitting beside the cart driver.

He thought about how to make a warning sound. A sound to tell Yip that danger was coming and that he and his pack needed to leave.

You never really forget the first language you learned. Twee barked at Yip. A different bark than Yip had used at first. This one was a warning, an urgent warning.

Yip trotted off toward his pack, gazing back at Twee as he went.

He wasn't moving fast enough for Twee, who could hear the cart noises getting louder, so Twee barked again, even more urgently this time.

Yip herded his pack off into the underbrush, turning for one last look at Twee as they disappeared.

Twee might have seen the love in Yip's eyes if he could have seen clearly through the tears trickling down from his own.

# 4

Thor started Twee on nails. "A good blacksmith cares about the quality of everything he makes, even something as simple as a nail," he said. Twee had watched Thor make nails and other things many times, but he was very excited to be standing on the other side of the forge this time.

Thor operated the bellows and even stoked the charcoal as Twee was the only apprentice. Twee had often wondered why he and Thor were alone in the smithy. Most blacksmith shops in the craftsman's district had multiple apprentices and several journeymen.

Thor hadn't answered, though he frowned when Twee asked the question.

The first piece was the nail header, the tool he would use to make the nails. He could have used a nail header Thor had forged, but making his own header would mean the nails would really be his own work.

Twee cut the raw iron bar to the correct size with a hot cut chisel, then hammered it flat with Thor watching his every move. Trying for precise hammer strikes, Twee defined the tool's head, then drew out the handle.

The header required a steel face to hold up to repeated use. Twee cut the steel to fit the header's front, then welded the steel onto the iron. He punched a hole in the header and quenched it (cooled in water to bring it back to room temperature and harden the metal). Twee was now ready to use his new nail header to make his first nail.

Taking the nail rod (a rod of iron just slightly wider than the hole Twee had punched in the header), Twee hammered the end out into a point. He tapered the end of the nail rod above the point with the hammer on the anvil until it slid smoothly into the nail header. Then he notched the rod above where it would stick out of the header and broke it off. Several quick hammer blows turned the end of the rod that stuck out of the header into a nail head.

Excitedly, Twee quenched the first nail he ever made and turned proudly to Thor.

Thor took the nail, put it on the anvil, and tapped it with his hammer. It shattered.

“You don’t quench a nail,” he said. “You need to let them cool naturally. If you quench them, they become too hard and brittle. A nail needs to be a little soft, so it won’t break like that.”

“Don’t fret, son,” he continued. “Aside from the quenching, that was good work. I’ve seen journeymen have more trouble forging nails.”

Twee started looking for Vix, the street urchin he had seen in the alley behind the shop when he ate lunch. He was a little worried about her, considering the urgency with which she ate the bread and cheese he had given her. Also, he liked the shy smile she had shown when she left.

He saw her again a few weeks later.

She walked down the alley just as he bit into his bread and cheese. Twee smiled to himself, broke his lunch in half, and tried to get her attention.

As with most of the street urchins in Grisput, trying to avoid attention was a big part of what she did. But Twee wasn’t a Grisput guard or a king’s man, and she remembered him, or at least his lunch.

She walked over to Twee and carefully took the food he offered her.

“Vix,” said Twee, “right?”

She looked startled that he remembered her, but she replied, “Twee.”

She was dressed in the same grimy burlap smock she had been wearing last time. Her hair might have been a bit longer, but it was still roughly cropped, tangled, and dirty.

Twee remembered and noticed all the pockets in the smock again.

As Vix stuffed the bread and cheese into her mouth, seemingly all in one bite, Twee tried to make small talk.

"Why so many pockets?" he asked.

Vix tried to respond, but her mouth was so full of bread and cheese all Twee could hear was mumbling. He held out his hand, palm outward, in a gesture that was supposed to convey patience.

Vix chewed for a moment, then said, "I have things. I need places to keep my things."

She tilted her head down a little, smiled at him again, whispered, "Thank you for the bread," and walked away down the alley.

Her smile and the whisper stuck in Twee's head even after she was long gone.

# 5

Twee ran an errand for Thor. It was a supply run this time. He had already handed the list to the man behind the counter. The man couldn't be bothered to even look at Twee, but he took the list and started to collect things from shelves.

"You're apprenticed to Thor Wodenswold, aren't you," the shopkeeper commented, again without glancing at Twee. He started to climb a ladder to reach something on the list that was on a higher shelf.

"Yes, sir," said Twee.

"You know, son," the shopkeeper called out from up the ladder. "You don't have to work for that northern barbarian. There are plenty of civilized blacksmiths in town who are eager for apprentices."

Twee didn't know how to respond to this.

The shopkeeper finished collecting the things on the list and returned to the front of the shop. He started putting the items on the counter in front of Twee.

"Just think about what I...," the shopkeeper looked at Twee for the first time. He noticed Twee's clipped ear, and his tone changed.

"Just give me what you owe me, and get out," he said.

Twee had been working with Thor for a year. He had gone from a boy who, though fit from his outdoor lifestyle, looked like a skinny forest animal to a young apprentice blacksmith. The hours of working the hammer, pumping the bellows, and lugging water, charcoal, and iron had given him some respectable upper body strength. He had also grown. He still had some way to go to reach a man's height. But, he was too tall to be thought of as a boy any longer.

He didn't let his hair grow long anymore. It was a danger in the forge to have long hair. Instead, he cut it short himself. It was a bit uneven but still the warm walnut brown it had always been. His short hair curled up in ringlets.

Some of the girls in the neighborhood noticed him—daughters of other craftsmen, young bondswomen, and even some older women in the district. Many of them wouldn't give him a second look once they noticed the clipped ear, but this wasn't the case with all of them.

Twee didn't know what to make of this. When some woman from the neighborhood flirted with him, his first instinct was to come up with some excuse for why he needed to get back to the forge to help Thor with something.

Twee enjoyed the lunches where Vix came by while he ate, however. He watched for her, and a lunch that he didn't get to split with Vix was an incomplete lunch.

One day as they were munching on bread and cheese on the stoop, he told her that.

"Vix," he said. "I wait for you at lunchtime. I miss you when you don't come by."

Vix had started sitting next to Twee as she ate. She looked at him and replied, "Sometimes, I'm busy."

She started searching through the pockets of her smock. Twee hadn't noticed before that some were bigger than others. She pulled something out of one of the smaller ones and handed it to him.

It was a dirty piece of string tied in a loop. A round lump of something shaped like a medallion was attached to the cord. It seemed it was made of dirt, but it was solid, and there wasn't any soil flaking off it. The earth, and whatever else was in the medallion, was polished somehow, such that it looked smooth, like a dirt gem.

"What's this?" Twee asked.

"It's me," Vix replied. "If you squeeze it, I'll know. It has some of my hair in it and some other things. You can wear it.

That's what the string is for."

Twee hung the string around his neck.

"My mother taught me how to make it," she concluded.

# 6

Thor and Twee were at the forge. Twee was pumping the bellows, and Thor was smithing an iron hinge at the anvil. It was a stag-horn hinge. Twee admired the process as the stag's head took shape under Thor's hammer's delicate, precise blows.

They were having a conversation, though, unlike some conversations, they conducted this one at a yelling volume with pauses for hammer blows and roars from the forge flames.

"I was talking to Maria," yelled Thor. "She says I shouldn't train you up to a journeyman."

He tapped with his hammer, using his chisel to separate the iron into two branches for a split in the stag's horn.

"Why not," yelled Twee.

Thor started flattening out part of the hinge to form the stag's face.

"She says you'll grow up and take my job."

Twee shook his head.

"I won't do that," he yelled.

Thor left the stag's face and started rolling the hinge barrel.

"Is that a promise, son?" he said with a wink. "You won't take my job, not until I ask you to?"

Twee watched as Thor curled the hinge barrel to fit the hinge pin.

"Not until you ask me to," he said.

Twee walked the cart down the main street of the craftsman's district. He felt good. The sun was shining, and the weather was warm. Thor was talking about letting him try his hand at a horseshoe.

He was leading the mules drawing the cart to the charcoal-burner. The burner lived inside the city walls, though he spent most of his time outside the walls at his charcoal kiln. His residence and shop were just at the district's edge, almost in the slums. (If you asked Maria, she might have drawn the boundary line for the slums on this side of his residence, perhaps partly because he lived there.)

The charcoal-burner was necessary. He supplied the smiths, glass-makers, and jewelry workers with vital charcoal. But there was something dirty and dark about his profession, and few wanted to live near him.

Even the skeptical and suspicious looks from the guardsmen who passed didn't break Twee's mood. A bondy leading a cart down the street by himself was an unusual and unwanted sight.

One of the people trudging by caught Twee's eye. It was Reynard. He hadn't seen Twee. He looked tired and wore a bondy's chains.

Twee pulled the mules to a stop, dropped the lead, and ran to Reynard. Startled, Reynard looked up. Twee drew Reynard to himself and hugged him.

"Twee?" said Reynard. He pushed Twee away a little and looked around at the busy street. "I'm glad to see you too, son," he said. "But you've got to be careful. The wrong person sees that, and they could get the wrong idea."

Reynard looked exhausted. Twee remembered what the constant wearing of chains was like and understood why.

"I'm just so happy to see you, Reynard," he said.

"Me too," said Reynard. He looked Twee up and down. "You look good, kid," he said. "You look like you won the bondy lottery."

"I'm doing all right," said Twee. "I'm apprenticed to a blacksmith."

"Apprenticed?" said Reynard.

Reynard was running an errand for his bond-holder. He

wasn't let out much, and even though wearing the chains while traveling any distance was tiring, he was still happy to be out on this one.

"I've got to get going, Twee," he said. "I'm pleased to see you, but I can't be late getting back. I didn't win the bondy lottery like you. You'd think with the number of spins I've had on the wheel..."

Twee gripped Reynard's shoulder.

"Keep your head down, Reynard," he said.

# 7

Twee was forging a horseshoe. "Horseshoes are usually made by a farrier, but a good blacksmith knows how to make everything a good blacksmith knows how to make. A smith is a smith," Thor said.

Twee was forging an iron shoe. "A steel shoe will last longer, but they're more difficult to smith and more expensive, so we mostly make iron ones," said Thor.

Starting with a piece of bar stock, Twee cut off a length that was fifteen inches long. He marked the center of the inside of the iron, so he wouldn't lose track of it while forging the shoe.

He shaped the stock with careful hammer blows into the shoe's curved shape using the anvil's horn.

Once he had the basic shape, he added the fullers, the creases along the shoe's center where the farrier would place the nails.

After adding the toe and heel nail holes and another in-between, he shaped the shoe's toe so the horse wearing it wouldn't stumble.

Thor nodded with approval when Twee finished. "I could have done better myself, but I've been wielding a hammer since before you were born."

"Hey, son," he said. "You won't take my job, not until I ask you to, right?"

"Not until you ask me to," said Twee.

Twee and Vix were sharing their lunch on the stoop. Vix was staring at Twee's clipped ear.

"Does that hurt?" she said.

Twee laughed. "It healed a long time ago," he said. Then, aware that the way Vix thought, this might not answer her question, he continued, "No, it doesn't hurt."

Vix looked at Twee and then started scanning through her pockets. She pulled out a little vial. At first, it surprised Twee she had such a thing. It was a small perfume bottle, the sort a great lady from the upper city might have. It didn't look like something a street urchin from the craftsman's district would own. Then he noticed a crack in the glass. It hadn't broken enough that it didn't seal, but a clearly visible fracture ran down the side of the bottle. Just the kind of thing that would make a great lady from the upper city discard it as imperfect.

Vix opened the bottle, shook it, and dabbed a little of the fluid inside on her finger. She quickly reached out and wiped it onto the missing part of Twee's earlobe. It stung like the devil.

"Loki's lewd linens!" said Twee. He was listening too much to Thor. "What the devil was that?"

"It's just some gunk," Vix said. "I call it 'Mama's spit.' It might help."

"Help with what?" said Twee. "What's in that?" he continued.

"Just some of my saliva ...," she looked thoughtful and continued, "maybe I shouldn't tell you what else."

Vix smiled shyly and proudly at the same time.

"My mother taught me how to make it."

# 8

When Twee woke the following morning, his ear was still stinging. For a minute, he was annoyed at Vix. He had no idea what she had put on his ear, but he didn't think it could be good if it was still hurting. Then he put his hand to his ear and realized his earlobe had grown back.

His next thought was panic. He couldn't imagine what the guards would do to a bondy who tried to hide his status by healing his ear. It couldn't be anything good.

He darted to his feet. He had a bit of time, as he was always first to rise. He was still sweeping the forge the first thing in the morning each day.

Twee got some lard from the kitchen and went to the forge for some soot. He mixed the two and smeared the mixture onto the place where the cut in his earlobe should be. Maria tried to decorate with as much class and style as their modest income would allow. One extravagance she felt made the home look more respectable was a polished bronze looking-glass hung in the hall.

Twee used the looking glass to make the black grease smear look like the missing earlobe as much as possible. People didn't look closely at a bondy's cut ear anyway. Once they realized it was cut, they would avoid looking there, like how you avoid seeing a cripple's injury.

Twee was forging an arrowhead. He was working with steel for the first time.

"Weapons are usually made by a weaponsmith, but a good blacksmith knows how to make everything a good blacksmith knows how to make. A smith is a smith," Thor said.

Twee was forging a broadhead arrowhead. Thor had given

him the choice of the broadhead or the bodkin, and he chose the broadhead.

Twee started by heating the end of a steel rod. He then flattened the end into a spoon shape to create the flat steel that he would form into the socket for the arrow shaft. He used delicate taps of the hammer to roll the flattened metal into a tube. Then he used a point mandrel to shape the socket correctly. He cut off one inch of the bar, careful not to damage the socket, and then drew the point out, keeping it rounded until he was ready to flatten the end to create the head.

After grinding and then treating it, Twee had an arrowhead he was proud of.

"Hey, son," Thor smiled as he spoke. "You won't take my job, not until I ask you to, right?"

"Not until you ask me to," said Twee.

The one thing Twee envied Baldur, aside from his non-bondy status, was school. Baldur was dragged to school each morning, protesting bitterly.

Twee, of course, started each morning by sweeping the smithy. Working with Thor was an education, but he missed the reading, writing, and arithmetic he had gotten from Anne.

There was, of course, no school for the bondys.

# 9

Twee was crafting his journeyman project. Thor gave him the choice of what he wanted to make, and he chose a dagger. He had been working with Thor for two years. Thor had decided it was time, and he was skilled enough to transition to journeyman smith.

Twee started by drawing an outline of how he wanted to shape the blade. Thor explained that there were many knife shapes and helped him pick the one he wanted for his project.

Twee rejected the baselard, as it was more of a cutting dagger, less useful for non-fighting utility purposes. He decided to craft a rondel dagger.

Twee started from a piece of tool steel from the scrap bin. Forging the knife blade from tool steel meant it would be a little susceptible to rust if he didn't take care of it. Twee hoped someday to wear this knife on his belt again, and once that was the case, he planned to take care of it like it was a part of him. Of course, as a bondy, wearing it on his belt was out of the question.

Twee cut the steel to the right shape and set about the forging of the blade. With the crafting of a dagger, there were multiple steps. After forging the metal into the right thickness and shape, Twee started grinding the edge. A time-consuming but vital piece of the crafting of this tool.

The handle was carefully carved from wood. Twee spent what seemed an inordinate amount of time, to Thor, on the handle carving, but in the end, when he put it all together, he had a blade to be proud of.

Crafted into the oiled and polished wood of the dagger's pommel was a wolf's head. It was carved by someone who didn't do much wood carving but took a lot of time to get it as right as possible. It would have just been a wolf to most people, but Twee tried as best he could to give it the features of a specific wolf. Twee tried as best as he could to make the pommel of his dagger have the face of Misha, his mother.

Thor nodded when he saw the finished knife.

With a serious expression on his face, Thor said, "You won't take my job, not until I ask you to, right?"

"Not until you ask me to," said Twee.

Twee started rubbing and playing with the medallion Vix had given him when he went to the back stoop to eat lunch. It was just a nervous habit. She began showing up more often to join him for lunch, and he was happy about that. On days when he ate on the stoop and she didn't show up, she apologized the next time he saw her.

"What's that on your ear?" she said one day. She no longer ate what he gave her as if someone was about to take it away from her, but she still ate it as if she wasn't sure where her next meal was coming from otherwise.

Vix wasn't a bondy. Since she was small, she had lived on the streets and had never been in bond service.

"I need to hide that my ear isn't clipped anymore. If someone sees that, I could get in trouble. I've been mixing soot and lard and putting it there to make it look like it's still cut."

Vix frowned. "It doesn't look very believable," she said. She ruffled through her pockets and came up with a small clay pot. It didn't have a lid, and like the perfume bottle he had seen before, it was cracked. It had a bit of something gray and greasy at the bottom.

"Mix a little of that in with the lard and soot," she said. "It might help."

Very matter-of-factly, she said, "My mother taught me how to make it."

# 10

Twee unloaded the charcoal and stabled the mules. He rubbed them down quickly before heading back to the forge. As he opened the door to the smithy, something felt wrong. He stepped inside and looked around.

Everything was in disarray. Someone had gone around the smithy, deliberately smashing and destroying everything they could. There was a pool of water in one area where a water trough had toppled. The bins of iron and steel scrap were overturned. Pieces of firewood were all over the floor that he swept each morning. Someone had taken the time to scatter the smithing tools all over the place, though they were difficult to destroy, so it might be just a matter of picking them up.

Worst of all, and most immediately in need of attention, somebody had scattered charcoal near the still burning forge. The fire was spreading from the lit forge to the coal scattered on the floor. It was approaching one of the support beams. If the wood of the support beam caught, the entire building could go up in flames.

Not all the water troughs were overturned, and Twee located a bucket that wasn't smashed. He managed to get the fire out by dumping buckets of water on it. Then he cleared the unburnt charcoal away from the forge and damped the fire.

Only then did he wonder where Thor was.

Thor was in one corner of the smithy, behind one of the ceiling support pillars. He lay on his back, his head resting against the wall. He smiled weakly as Twee approached. One arm lay at his side. The other was under his blacksmith's apron.

In a wavering voice, he said as Twee approached, "Good job with the fire, son, I knew I could count on you."

"Are you all right, Thor? What happened?"

"It was just some kids," Thor replied softly. "Saying things about barbarians. They were trying to cause trouble."

As Twee got closer, he noticed a deep gash in Thor's apron. He leaned down next to Thor and lifted the apron.

"It was just a seax. Like you made, Twee. I knew I should have worn my thicker apron today."

The hand Thor held under the apron was covered in blood and was pressed firmly into his gut. There was blood soaking his shirt and in a puddle beneath him.

"It was just a little thing, not a real weapon like an ax or a hammer. I'm surprised it made it through the apron. I'll be fine." Thor sighed.

# 11

Thor was laid up in his room. Twee tried to finish the jobs coming due, but working alone was challenging. He attempted to talk to the healers and Maria about what was happening with Thor, but they didn't think it was a bondy's place to be involved.

He tried to find a way to eavesdrop secretly. Eventually, he managed to be in the right place at the right time to overhear Maria talking to a healer.

"If it hadn't been for the apron, he'd be dead already," said the healer.

"Are you sure there's nothing more you can do today?" said Maria.

"I'm not sure my medicines will work the same way on one of these northerners," said the healer. "But I've done everything I can, anyway."

Twee could imagine Maria's face in response to this comment.

There was a moment of silence.

"I'm sure his strong constitution will allow him to pull through," said the healer.

The next day, Maria came to Twee in the smithy and told him Thor wanted to talk to him. Twee went to Thor's bed. Either Maria respected the conversation enough to leave them alone or didn't want to be in the room. Either way, it was just the two of them.

Thor lay in his bed. Twee looked around briefly. He had lived in this house for three years, but he hadn't been in this room before.

"Twee," Thor said weakly from the bed. "Come here."

Twee approached the bed. Thor looked pale.

"Twee," said Thor, "I've talked to Maria. I need your help with something. Maria and Baldur don't have any source of income except the smithy. I need you to run the smithy."

"Thor," said Twee, "you know I can't do that. I'm a bondy. No one will work with me."

"Maria will talk to our customers and suppliers. Some of them will refuse, but hopefully, enough will go along to keep things running for a while. She'll buy a cheap young bondy for you as an apprentice."

Thor held a handkerchief to his mouth and coughed. Twee noticed that even his cough sounded frail.

"Twee," said Thor. "Please. I need this."

Thor smiled weakly.

"You won't take my job, will you, Twee, not until I ask you to?"

"Not until you ask me to," said Twee in a shaking voice.

# 12

Twee wasn't allowed to go to the funeral. He wasn't sure he would have wanted to go, anyway. The funeral wasn't for him, nor for Thor. It was for Maria and Baldur. The cemetery was outside the city walls, so Twee couldn't even visit Thor's grave. That he would have wanted to do.

Maria did what Thor asked and bought a young bondy to help Twee with the smithing. He wasn't much use, though Twee imagined that he hadn't been much use at first, either. His name was Aylmer, and while he was capable of pumping the bellows and hauling charcoal and water, that was about it.

It was enough, however, for the most part. Twee was able to finish the outstanding jobs, and though the number of new orders was reduced, there were still some coming in.

Twee set up a cot for himself in the corner of the smithy. He wanted Aylmer to have his own space, and he also wanted to maintain a little distance from Maria and Baldur.

Life settled into a routine. Twee established a set of customers who didn't object to working with a bondy smith and figured out which suppliers would work with him. The number of jobs was less than when Thor ran the smithy, but that was a good thing in some ways, as it allowed Twee to keep up.

Some jobs were difficult for Twee. Things Thor hadn't taught him. He'd been watching Thor work for years, but watching Thor do something was different from doing it himself. Twee did the best he could.

The highlight of Twee's day was when he got to eat lunch with Vix. Aylmer tried to join them one time, but Twee gave him a dirty look. He left and found himself another place to eat.

Twee started going to a local pub some evenings to have

an ale. The pub was called "The Captive Wolf." The carved wooden sign over the door showed an iron animal trap, like the one that killed Ulmer.

When Twee first saw the sign and heard the name, he was reluctant to enter the pub, but it was the closest to the forge and the one where he got the fewest dirty looks when he walked in.

Twee went to the pub alone when he went. He would sit in the corner, order one ale, and drink it. The regulars grew to recognize and accept him and left him alone to enjoy his drink.

Sometimes it seemed they enjoyed having him there. He became a bit of a celebrity or, at least, a feature: the bondy who ran his own business. Sometimes he could tell they were talking about him. He ignored them and just drank his ale.

# 13

One evening while Twee sat quietly in the corner of "The Captive Wolf," nursing the last drops of his ale, the door burst open, and several of the king's guards entered the pub. The heads of all the patrons turned toward them.

The king's men were a bit of an unusual sight in Grisput. City business that required armed presence was usually taken care of by the Grisput guards.

The captain stepped into the center of the open area in the middle of the pub and loudly announced, "Is there a man in this pub named Twilight?"

He was a man with an air of authority, and no one thought about refusing him his request, but the answer he got was a muttered chorus of noes and denials.

The captain frowned and leaned his head toward another king's man, who whispered something into his ear.

"How about 'Twi'?" he said.

Half the heads in the pub turned toward Twee.

"You there," said the captain, gesturing toward Twee. "Come here."

Twee rose and walked toward the captain. In the last year, he had gotten so tired of endlessly submitting to disrespect and contempt that he stood as straight and proud as he could, looked the captain right in the eye, and said, "My name is Twee, Sir."

It was a good thing for Twee that he was facing a king's guardsman and not one of the Grisput Guard. A Grisput guardsman would never have put up with that kind of disrespect from a bondy. The captain nodded at Twee and said, "Close enough."

"I arrest this man in the name of the prince regent," said the captain. One of the guardsmen stepped up behind Twee and grabbed his wrists. The guardsman who had whispered in his captain's ear said, "We should pay off his bond-holder to keep things simpler."

Twee gaped.

"What did I do?" he asked.

"Not my concern," said the captain.

There was an unusual amount of action in the street just outside "The Captive Wolf" pub that evening. Neighbors and passersby got an eyeful when they stood watching. Two entire squads of the king's men were bustling around and loading several carts for a trip. The whispering crowds were convinced they had caught a wanted criminal and were ready to transport him to the capital. The whispers and speculation got even more eager when one of the guardsmen was sent off to the door of the barbarian blacksmith's wife.

There was a transaction there that involved an exchange of money.

"I knew she was up to no good," said Alyssa, the goldsmith's wife. "Marrying that barbarian."

Ada Hempleman leaned close to Alyssa, so the other women from the neighborhood wouldn't hear the secret she whispered in the loudest stage whisper she could manage. "You know her bondy has been running the smithy," she said.

"So that's who they arrested," said Alyssa.

"I knew it was illegal for a bondy to run a business," said Ada with satisfaction.

The carts started off down the street, rumbling over the cobbles.

If they had watched more carefully and talked a bit less, they might have noticed a small figure slip through the shadows toward the caravan. They might have seen the shape, dressed entirely in burlap, disappear behind a case in the luggage storage area on the back of the last cart.

# FALCON

# 1

In the northwest corner of the kingdom of Liamec, nestled in the foothills of the Etenies Mountains, was a lake. This body of water might have had a name, but it wasn't used. People who lived near enough to the lake to speak of it referred to it as "The Lake." There were two towns on the lake. On the west side was Ashton, and on the east was Lakeside.

There was an island in the lake near Ashton. This island was sometimes called the isle of the wise and sometimes called the isle of fools by people who weren't convinced of the whole thing's wisdom.

Around Ashton and on the isle of the wise were places, buildings, and people, which constituted an academy. Like "The Lake," this academy was referred to simply as "The Academy." It was the place where magic was officially studied and learned by the people of Liamec.

For many years, the Academy trained its students in four disciplines of magic. Alchemy, channeling, illusion, and elements. A fifth discipline has been taught for the last few years: clairvoyance. Clairvoyance was still controversial, and some aspects of the best ways to study, use, and survive its use were still uncertain. But it was becoming apparent it was potent and powerful in its applications.

One of the better-known practitioners of clairvoyance was a woman named Clarissa. After graduating from the Academy with her clairvoyance skills, she set up shop in Lakeside as a consulting clairvoyant.

Her predictions were expensive, confusing, and obscure, but they were always right. Due to the confusion and the obscurity, sometimes you didn't know they were right until after the fact, and occasionally not even then, but they were always right.

You could ask Clarissa a question if you desired, for a price, and then try your best to see if you could understand the answer. Clarissa also sometimes came up with predictions or prophecies, which she would try to sell to the person or persons who might find them most useful.

Part of the confusion and obscurity of Clarissa's predictions was due to the discipline's very nature. The Academy had not yet solved all the issues the study of clairvoyance had, one of which was insanity.

It might not be described as full-blown insanity. The study of clairvoyance seemed to open the student's mind to things beyond just knowledge of the future. It became difficult to have a normal conversation with a clairvoyant. Asking a clairvoyant what time it was, for example, could open up a discussion of the nature of time. This discussion could quickly become too deep for the average person and would rarely answer the original question.

Asking for a clarification of a prophecy could yield an answer which was more obscure and challenging than the original prediction.

A few months ago, Clarissa gave a complex and detailed prediction that her handlers decided needed government attention. Sending an urgent message to the prince regent left Clarissa with a welcome and handsome payment. It had also left the prince regent and his household with a challenging conundrum.

# 2

Twee woke up. For a moment, he didn't know where he was. It was dark, and the only trace of light came from a small high window on the other side of the room. This wasn't the smithy where he had slept for the last year.

He sat up, shook himself, and realized that he still didn't know where he was even with the complete arrival of consciousness.

Oh, he knew enough to know he was in a cell in a dungeon somewhere. He knew enough to know that the small slice of light was coming into the cell through a barred window high in a heavy oak door. He knew enough to know it was flickering torchlight, not sunlight.

Twee remembered the last time he had found himself locked in a cell. The memories were fuzzy, partly because it was so long ago and partly because he'd been a different person back then-if he'd been a person at all. He remembered the sound of Anne's voice. From when she spoke to him in that cell and from a thousand different times when she helped him or had taken care of him.

Twee sat on the stuffed-straw pallet he had slept on and cried for a moment. Then he pulled himself together. What would Thor do? What would Bear do? They wouldn't be sitting here crying.

The carts had rumbled out of Grisput, through country roads, into and out of towns for several days. Twee was locked into a prison cart with little light and no way to see out. He hadn't been badly treated, though he was largely ignored, and no one responded to his questions.

Twee hadn't even been sure which direction they were

taking him, though he would have speculated that they were mainly traveling north if he'd had to guess.

When they reached their destination, the cart rumbled to a stop on cobblestones. The guardsmen opened the door and dragged Twee out, blinking, into the bright daylight. He had just enough time to get a quick impression of his surroundings before they led him on.

The cart had stopped in a cobbled courtyard of a massive stone castle. Twee couldn't get a complete picture of its scale from his glimpse, but there were stone walls and towers as far as he could see. The only thing Twee had to compare it to was the walls of Grisput, and while the walls and towers he could see weren't higher than the walls of Grisput, they might out extend them.

The guards bundled Twee through a door, along endless wide branching stone corridors, and down aging stone staircases. He tried at first to keep track of which way to go or which turn to take if he needed to retrace the route, but it was an intricate labyrinth, and he had no chance to hold it in his mind.

The thudding of the heavy wooden door slamming shut left Twee alone in the dark with nothing but his thoughts.

He had never felt more alone.

# 3

Two guards came for Twee sometime later. The light coming in through the narrow barred window in the door was torchlight, so he didn't know what time of day it was or how much time had passed.

They grabbed him and manacled his arms behind his back. The trek through the maze of corridors was just as confusing as last time. They kept walking for so long Twee couldn't understand how they could be in the same building.

After a time, there came a transition. It was like in the forest, when you change altitude or move from one part of the forest into another. The nature of the vegetation changes, and with it, the entire feel of the environment. They transitioned from the castle's underbelly, where the servants and guardsmen lived and worked, to the upper rooms, where things were more rarefied.

Now, there were elegant tapestries on the walls. The servants were in a hurry to get from one place to another. There were carpets on the floors in many rooms. The lighting improved. No more flickering torches; lamp sconces graced the walls in rooms without outside lighting. There was even glass in some windows.

The guardsmen, one holding each of his arms, dragged Twee through double doors into a vast ornate room, pulled him forward onto a crimson section of carpet, and forced him to his knees.

"Kneel in the presence of the prince regent," one of them hissed.

Twee knelt on the carpet. He felt it was best to keep his eyes down, but he snuck a quick glimpse before looking away. If Twee hadn't been trying to maintain the illusion that he was averting his gaze, his mouth would have gaped open. He wasn't kneeling in front of a man but a god.

Twee had heard of the prince regent, of course, in Grisput. He hadn't been part of many political conversations, but he overheard people talking sometimes. The prince regent: sometimes called the young regent and sometimes the Young Lion. He ruled for the old king, King Liam III, who was infirm enough to be incapable.

The young prince had been ruling as regent for ten years. When they were sure their conversation wasn't being overheard by the wrong people, people would curse him. Excessive taxation, lawlessness, and guard abuses were all laid at his feet. The people of Grisput thought of the Young Lion and his capital as very far away, but his laws and policies still had a bearing on them.

Twee found it hard to hold those thoughts in his head, kneeling in front of the man. He was magnificent. He was young, less than ten years older than Twee, tall, healthy, and handsome. He was the image of everything a king should be.

The Lion was dressed in a purple velvet doublet and tight gray leggings. He wore a grand glittering gold medallion, which reflected and diffracted the sunlight from the tall windows on the side of the chamber into rainbows and flashing beams of brilliance.

Framing his face was a luxurious mane of tawny blond hair braided into a plait as wide as his head that flowed down to just below his shoulders.

He looked down at Twee, kneeling before him, and his perfect face formed into a sneer. Twee looked at the expression, and even though it was focused on him, he felt full of disdain, himself, for whoever the target of that expression might be.

The Young Lion looked down on Twee and said, "So, guttersnipe, I hear you claim to be my cousin."

Twee carefully looked up. If the prince regent's magnificent presence hadn't been enough to overawe him, the throne room would have done it by itself.

There was a massive ornate throne set against the wall behind the Lion. It looked golden, though the blacksmith in Twee, who knew something of metals and their properties, felt sure it couldn't be pure gold. The wall behind and above the throne was broken up by several tall stained glass windows showing scenes in glorious colors, depicting events from the history of Liamec.

A broad strip of crimson carpet ran from the double doors down the middle of the room. The carpet reached the throne dais and continued up the stairs to the throne's base. The room was longer than it was wide, allowing one to approach the throne slowly down the middle. The walls on both sides had high windows. On one side, the morning sunshine was spilling into the room, leaving puddles of sunlight that flowed horizontally across the carpet and the stone floor near the walls.

Twee, the guards who brought him, and the young regent were the only people in the room.

The regent didn't seem to wait for a response to his comment, but there was a silence, an awkward moment, where no one spoke. Twee had no idea what to say or if he should say anything. This place and this presence were so out of touch with any experience he'd had in his life he couldn't process it. It was clear the guards were not going to speak. This was the regent's moment, and he felt no need to put anyone at their ease. He didn't seem bothered by the silence.

Twee started to open his mouth to say something.

The regent interrupted Twee's attempt to speak by turning to one of the guards and saying, "It can't even talk. There is no way this thing is related to me."

The Young Lion wasn't really talking to the guard. The guard was just a convenient target for his orders and comments. It was the room, in general, that was being addressed. He looked through the guard and spoke to the surrounding space. There was a clear understanding that what he said would be made to happen when he spoke to the room.

"Take it back to the dungeons and lock it up." He paused as if in thought.

"Don't go easy on it, however," he continued. "I want it treated harshly. Don't give it two blankets, just one, and don't give it cake.

"It doesn't deserve cake."

# 4

Twee was back in his cell. The cell felt almost familiar and comfortable after his talk with the regent. He tried to process what had just happened. They wouldn't let him speak. If someone, anyone, would talk to him and let him respond, he could explain. They needed to send him back to Grisput. Orders were coming due, and there was no way Aylmer could complete them. This business the regent spoke about was just a misunderstanding. He missed the smithy. He missed his daily routine. He missed lunches with Vix.

Twee reached into his shirt and held the little dirt medallion Vix had given him. He lifted the charm out and rubbed it against his face. He had never figured out how something made of dirt was polished to be so smooth and shiny. He'd asked Vix once, but her reply was only that her mother had taught her how to make it.

There was a noise on the other side of the door. It had to be the guards coming back. Maybe this time, they would take him to someone who would listen to him while he tried to explain. Twee went and sat on the bed.

The slight sound from outside the cell grew a little louder. It sounded like a person whispering. Twee thought it was someone whispering his name. He stood and walked over to the door. He heard a clear and urgent whisper from the other side. The window was high enough that he couldn't see through it.

He recognized the voice. It was Vix.

"Freya's Frozen Fur," Twee almost shouted.

"Quiet, Twee," came the voice from the other side of the door. "I'm not sure how far away the guards are."

More quietly, Twee continued, "Vix, how did you get here? Where are you sleeping? How did you find me?"

"Are you hungry, Twee?" said Vix calmly.

Twee hadn't thought about it in a while. The interview with the prince regent had driven thoughts of anything else out of his head. He was starving. They hadn't given him any food since yesterday, and contrary to what the regent had suggested, there was no cake. The food they provided him was meager, though enough to get by.

"Yes," he responded. Almost immediately, at the bottom of the barred window, he could see the corner of a piece of bread appear. He could imagine Vix on the other side of the door, standing on her tiptoes to hold the food up high enough for him to reach it through the window.

He reached up to grab it. It was two slices of bread, with some cheese in-between, just like they had eaten for lunch many times over the last few years. A couple of bites were missing from one side of the bread.

"Did you eat some of this, Vix?" he asked.

"I was hungry."

"They think I've been saying I'm related to the prince," Twee said.

"I've found a place behind an oven in the kitchens. No one looks back there, and it's warm.

"I don't have a way to get through this door," Vix continued. She sounded a little frustrated.

"Hold on, Twee," she said. "I'll be right back."

# 5

It was difficult to judge time in the cell. The flickering torchlight coming in through the window didn't change. There was a sound like a steady dripping of water. It wasn't coming from anywhere inside the cell, but it was the only thing he could hear other than his heartbeat. With these two sounds, he felt it should be possible to estimate time somewhat if he counted, but it was hard to focus.

There was a noise at the door. Twee was about to creep over, ready to whisper with Vix again-when it opened. It didn't burst or creak slowly open. It opened solemnly, like a door at a ballroom entrance swinging wide when guests were introduced.

Light blazed into the room, and Twee squinted in the sudden brightness.

"Her ladyship, the countess Olivia D'Arilo," came a polished voice.

A refined lady strode into the cell. Her only concession to the surroundings was a set of clips on the bottom edge of her dress that held it a few inches above the dirty stone floor.

She wore an elegant blue satin gown that would be better suited to a fancy drawing-room than a dungeon cell.

She looked old to Twee. Her hair was a delicate flaxen yellow, like sunlight reflecting off a haystack on a summer day. Though they were hard to detect, she had hints of gray in her hair. She had a sharp nose and a mouth that could change from a warm smile to a stern glower in a heartbeat.

It did that now. The lady smiled at Twee, then frowned at the cell.

"Lord Twilight," she said, holding her hand towards Twee, her fingertips turned downward.

Twee looked at the hand. He didn't know what to do. He

remembered Anne reading stories to him back in the outlaw camp. They sometimes had a gentleman kissing a lady's hand. Maybe this was the moment for that.

Feeling like he was making the biggest fool of himself he could, Twee reached out his hand and held it under hers. He didn't touch her hand for fear of the grime on his. He lowered his head and grazed the back of her hand with his lips, then he dropped his hand and took a step back.

She looked at him with a pleased look on her face. She might have had the same look if she encountered a stray dog, and it suddenly did an amusing trick.

Twee blinked. He noticed that other people had come into the cell. The countess D'Arilo had filled his attention so wholly they somehow snuck in without him perceiving them. There were quite a few people in the cell now. So many that the small space felt crowded.

The person who had announced the countess's entrance stood near the door. He was a multicolored popinjay, though the effect of his outfit's colors was somehow flamboyant without being gaudy.

There were several guardsmen. They wore uniforms similar in style to those of the king's men. As with the Grisput guard, they wore a different color tabard and emblem to differentiate themselves. The tabard was a shade of yellow, and on the center of the front was a black silhouette of a raptor bird's claw, open and grasping at something not pictured.

There were also two other men dressed in formal attire. They were very earnest and inspected the dungeon, taking notes in small books they carried.

The countess looked around the cell. The frown which Twee saw there earlier came back. It crossed Twee's mind that he was relieved that it wasn't directed at him.

"This will never do," she said as if to herself.

"Lord Twilight," she said to Twee. "Would you mind if we have a conversation somewhere other than here? I think we have much to talk about, you and I."

## 6

After Twee nodded, the countess swept out of the cell, gesturing to the guardsmen to bring him. Two of them stepped up beside Twee. No manacles or arms twisted behind his back this time; they walked beside him as they escorted him out of the cell and through the corridors. He thought that if he tried to bolt off down a hallway, they would have been after him in a moment, but he didn't feel the urge. This felt more like a rescue than a further ordeal. The only thing Twee regretted about leaving the cell was that he wouldn't be there when Vix came back.

They encountered the king's guard several times as they walked through the corridors and up the torch-lit stairwells. The first encounter was with guards who were clearly the main prison detail for the dungeons.

Each time, the yellow-clad guardsmen, the countess, the popinjay, and Twee waited while the formally attired gentlemen with the notebooks stepped forward.

Twee couldn't overhear what was said, but the gentlemen seemed to do a lot of talking. They also produced papers and formal documents from their bags. The guardsmen appeared confused initially but eventually agreed to let them pass in each case.

At the official dungeon guard post, it took longer. After arguing a while, the guardsmen called a superior. The group escorting Twee, and the guards, waited for him to arrive. After a bit more talking, they passed that test as well.

After what seemed an interminable trek, they passed into a different part of the castle. Twee kept waiting for when they would leave the corridors and step outside into a courtyard or leave one building for another, but that moment never came.

Gradually the guards they saw passing by in the corridors changed from king's men to yellow-tabarded guards similar to those traveling with them.

Finally, they swept into the fancy drawing-room Twee had imagined when the countess first graced his cell in the dungeon.

Several people in the room seemed to have been waiting for them. One was an older man with a flowing white beard. Twee almost laughed when he saw him. He wore a cone-shaped hat on his head, black, with yellow-painted stars and moons on it. He looked so much like a character from one of the stories Anne had read to Twee that Twee felt like he must be imitating him.

The man with the beard and hat stepped forward. The countess directed arrivals and departures. She tried to dismiss the guards with a hand gesture. The guards looked at each other as she did so, and while several left, one stayed behind. Twee noticed he maintained a discreet distance, but he seemed to keep his eye on Twee the entire time.

The countess released the formally attired gentlemen. Unlike the guards, who she had dismissed with a hand gesture, she was more careful with these men's dismissal. She thanked each one and graciously offered them her hand to kiss as they departed. Twee watched, and it occurred to him he hadn't done too poorly. In fact, he thought, his kiss had been better than at least one of these two.

The multicolored popinjay, a gentleman usher to the countess, took up a position by the door.

"Is this him?" said the man with the hat.

"Of course," said the countess. "Who did you think it would be?"

# 7

The countess looked Twee up and down. "Lord Twilight," she said. He blushed for a second under her attention, then he pulled himself together and stood as straight and proud as he could.

"Twee," said Twee. He was reluctant to interrupt, but he didn't know who Lord Twilight was, and he needed to clear up some of the confusion.

"Twee," she repeated. She looked puzzled for a second but continued.

"I have something difficult to ask of you," she said. "This gentleman," and she gestured toward the man in the hat. "Needs a small sample of your blood. Just a pinprick will do. It's not for anything nefarious, I promise you. Just a little test."

She looked directly into Twee's eyes as she said this, and at that moment, he would have found it difficult to refuse her anything.

Twee nodded. The man in the hat reached out, held Twee's arm for a second, and poked him with a needle he produced from somewhere. It didn't hurt much, but Twee had a second of worry. He had no idea what he had just agreed to.

The man scurried off, and the countess gestured to a chair.

"First things first," she said. "Normally, I would consider getting you into new clothes and getting you something to eat as the first things. But as I said, we have much to discuss, and we'll have to be barbarians for a moment."

Twee sat in one chair, and the countess alighted in another. The amount of grime on the seat of his britches briefly distracted Twee, but the countess had asked him to sit, so he did.

A lady who stood in the background, one of the people who had been waiting for them to arrive, stepped forward, hearing the countess's comment about barbarians. She was dressed in a simple linen dress, and Twee could tell by sight that she was a servant in the household. It was funny how you could tell which level in the castle someone occupied at just a glance.

She bobbed a curtsy and said, "With your permission, my lady."

The countess nodded, and the lady took out a measuring rod. She quickly and expertly ran the stick over Twee's body, ignoring his protests and flinches. She then left the room.

"Twee," said the countess. "Do you have questions, or do you want me to just start talking?"

Twee had so many questions he couldn't decide which ones to ask. He hesitated.

"All right," said the countess. "I'll start, and you can ask what you need as we go."

"First off," she began. "We just got you out of the prince regent's personal dungeons against his wishes. Not against his direct orders or against his express commands, but against his wishes. This is a dangerous thing."

She frowned and looked down at the elegant carpet which covered the drawing-room floor.

"I wouldn't have done this if I hadn't been worried you might disappear down there. The way we got you out was by using something called lawyers. You probably haven't heard about them; they are something new. Good King Liam III, before his decline, was a firm believer in law.

"A lawyer is a man who works with the laws. They learn about them, how they work, and how to use them to the advantage of their clients. The prince regent is not a strong believer in law; he would like to return to the old ways. The changes old king Liam implemented were robust enough to make it hard for him. The laws and the lawyers have staying power. That's one of the few things that's kept the regent from fully controlling the system. It's also why he's still regent and not king."

Twee nodded. Some of this made sense to a certain degree.

There was one big thing that still bothered him, however.

"What does this have to do with me, your ladyship?" he said.

# 8

The countess smiled. Twee felt a little warmer. "Well, Twee," she said, "Here is where I have a few questions for you. What do you know about your family? Your background? Specifically, your father?"

Twee shook his head.

"Nothing," he said. "I lost them when I was very young."

"Any names, a locket with a painting, anything?" the countess said.

"No," said Twee.

The countess sighed. "Well, we'll see what old stars-on-his-head comes up with," she laughed. The laugh was a pleasant thing. It made Twee smile to hear it.

The expression on the countess's face became more serious.

"Sorry, Twee, that was disrespectful. Forget I said it," she said.

"Anyway," she continued. "To answer your question, as best I can. Not too long ago, there was a prophecy. A clairvoyant named Clarissa from the Academy came up with a detailed vision. It was recorded and given to the prince regent. It mentions you. In several ways and places. In some ways, you could say the whole thing is about you."

"Me?" said Twee. The gaped mouth expression, haunting him a bit, came back.

"The prophecy contains a great deal of information. Some obscure, and some very specific and clear."

Twee tried to wrap his head around this. It still had to be a case of mistaken identity.

"Your ladyship," he said, trying to be as respectful as possible. "It must be a mistake. I'm no one important."

"One of the clearer things in the prophecy was where and when you could be found," the countess continued. "The wolf will be caught on the spring solstice in the city of the coiled serpent as the sun sets."

She frowned, "Unfortunately, the regent's men figured out the 'The wolf will be caught' referred to the 'The Captive Wolf' pub in Grisput before we did."

Twee was still trying. "That didn't have to be about me. There were other people in the pub," he said.

"By the time of day shall you know him. Twilight is his name, and twilight is his time. And, if he doesn't respond to that, try 'Twi.'"

Finally, something rang true to Twee. Since he first heard it, the name twilight felt right to him.

"But," he said. "If the prophecy was given to the regent, how do you know what was in it?"

"The regent isn't smart enough to figure out what it meant himself. He had people reading the text. Many people are concerned about how he's running the kingdom. Someone looking at it felt it was important that a copy of the text get into other hands than just the regent's."

The man in the hat made a gesture from the other side of the room, where he had a strange apparatus set up on a table.

"Just a minute, Twee," the countess said. She rose and swept across the floor toward the man. Someone had removed the clips from the bottom of her dress. The graceful swish of her passage over the drawing-room carpet was mesmerizing to Twee.

The countess approached the man. They were on the other side of the room, and perhaps they underestimated Twee's hearing. He was young, and his years of living with the wolves had honed it. He couldn't hear what the countess was saying, but the man was facing him, and his voice was loud enough. What Twee heard him say was, "A direct male descendant. The test shows it. I'd stake my Academy certification on it."

The countess returned to Twee.

"You must be tired," she said. "We've got rooms already prepared for you. I'm sure that something to eat and a good night's sleep will be just the ticket."

# 9

The guardsman who escorted Twee away from the drawing-room seemed more friendly. Perhaps Twee had passed a test by being welcomed by the countess. He felt he could try to strike up a conversation.

"Where are we going?" he said.

"As the countess said, there is a suite of rooms set aside for your use," said the guardsman, "It's in the ruby wing, not too far from her ladyship's own quarters."

"The ruby wing?" asked Twee.

"Her ladyship occupies the Ruby and Emerald wings of the King's Seat," the guardsman said proudly.

"The King's Seat?" said Twee.

"Were you raised in the woods?" said the guardsman incredulously. "Everyone knows about the King's Seat."

"I'm not everyone," said Twee sadly.

"Our regent," said the guardsman, and as he said this, an involuntary shiver seemed to run down his body, "has been working on the King's Seat since his regency began."

Twee was still confused and looked at the guardsman with the confusion clearly showing on his face.

The man sighed. "The King's Seat is the hereditary residence of the kings of Liamec. When the regent began his regency, perhaps to show he was king in all but name, he undertook a massive construction project to improve and expand the Seat. The Seat was already one of the biggest castles in Liamec. After the regent's first project finished, it was the largest. Everyone thought that would be enough, but he immediately ordered new plans, and new construction started."

The guardsman paused, drew a deep breath, and continued, "He's been working on the Seat ever since. It occupies most of the noble quarter of Capitol now. All the branches of government, and most of the nobility, have offices and/or living quarters in the King's Seat."

"They divided it up into wings a long time ago, so they had a way to refer to places within the castle. They had to number the suites and rooms to describe locations. Your suite of rooms, for example, is Ruby 45."

"Speaking of which," he said, "here we are." He stopped beside a sturdy oak door in the stone wall of the corridor and held the door open for Twee.

As Twee stepped inside, he heard the door thud closed behind him.

The room was enormous. It had high vaulted ceilings and windows showing the echoes of twilight fading from the sky. There were tapestries on the walls. There was a privacy alcove in the corner with its own privy. Twee had never seen such luxury. This room by itself was almost bigger than the entire interior of the smithy.

A steaming hot bathtub stood in the center of the room. The lady who had measured Twee earlier in the countess's drawing-room stood beside it.

Far be it from us to describe the horrors Twee underwent over the next hour. There was hair cutting, nail clipping, scrubbing, and clothes fitting. Not to mention other torments. Twee lost track of how many people entered and exited the room to foist additional indignities on him.

Somewhere during the process, they gave him something to eat. He wasn't sure how or when it had happened, but he could tell by the satisfied feeling in his belly.

By the time someone bundled him into a giant four-poster bed with a down mattress and comforter, he felt like he had lost several layers of skin. He tried to look for his clothes at one point, but they had been burned. He kept a tight hold of the amulet Vix gave him the whole time so they couldn't take it away and burn it as well.

Twee was so sound asleep that he almost didn't hear the knocking on the door. It was a quiet knock, but somehow it felt urgent enough to penetrate his sleeping brain. He crept out of his bed and over to the door. He wore a nightshirt. Like much of what happened last night, he didn't remember putting it on.

Twee tried the door. It was locked. As the doorknob rattled, he heard a whisper from outside.

"Twee?"

"Vix?" said Twee.

"Are you all right, Twee? I was worried about you," came Vix's voice.

"You were worried about me?" said Twee. "I was worried about you."

"Look under the door, Twee," said Vix. "I have something for you."

Twee looked under the door. There was just enough space for something slender to fit.

He saw a familiar face appear. It was the carved wooden face of Misha on the pommel of his tooth.

"Thanks, Vix," he said, pulling the dagger from under the door. "Where are you going to stay tonight? Are you going to be all right?"

"I'll be all right," she said. "Don't worry about me."

# 10

The countess installed Twee as a member of her household. She told people he was a nephew visiting from out of town. Town, by the way, was Capitol. Capitol was the city that had housed the kings of Liamec since the reign of Liam the first. It was said that when it was established, it had another name. That name fell into disuse, and you had to look on ancient maps or talk to a cartographer to find it. On more modern charts, the name Capitol was written, or sometimes just Cap.

Twee was given a wardrobe of custom-made clothes, set up in Ruby 45 for the long term, and told he had the run of the Ruby Wing's upper levels. When she told him this, the countess strongly encouraged Twee not to try to leave the wing.

"Most people in Capitol and in the King's Seat don't know who you are, but we wouldn't want you running into one of the regent's men. I managed to get you out of their clutches once. The regent wasn't expecting my tactics. I'm not sure I could do it again."

In exchange for all this largess and more luxury than Twee had ever known, the countess asked a few things of him. She wanted him to attend lessons. She would have various tutors brought in, and she wanted Twee to take classes with them. Twee didn't object to this. In fact, it was an additional improvement in his life to him. For the last several years, one of his sorrows had been that he couldn't attend school with Baldur in Grisput.

She also asked Twee to bide his time and not do anything rash. Twee really didn't know what she was asking him, so this was also an easy request to accede to. She hinted that she was sounding things out and would let him know when the time was suitable. Again, Twee wasn't sure what the time would be suitable for, so he kept his counsel.

Twee did take one chance. When a cobbler was fitting him for boots, he showed the cobbler his tooth and asked if he could put a concealed sheath into a boot. Twee was a little surprised by the cobbler's reaction. He acted like this was an absolutely reasonable request. It seemed he would have been surprised if Twee hadn't wanted a knife sheath in his boot. It made Twee wonder a little about life in the court of the prince regent.

Twee jumped up when he heard a knock on his door that evening. It was the first time he would be able to actually see Vix since they'd come to Capitol. They'd talked through locked doors a few times, but he looked forward to talking without a locked door between them.

He opened the door and looked into the stone-walled corridor. There was no one there. Then there was a stirring in the shadows, and Vix appeared. Twee reached out and pulled her to him. He took in her scent as he squeezed the grimy, faded burlap-covered shape against his clean white linen nightshirt. She smelled like rancid, slightly rotten fabric and moldy cheese. She smelled like home.

"Vix," he said. "We've got to introduce you to the countess. I think she'll let you live here."

"I already live here," Vix said. "They never check behind their ovens."

"But I think we can make it official," Twee said. "She's really nice.

"We'll have to get you cleaned up. At least a bit," Twee continued. "I think it's important to make a good first impression."

# 11

Twee went with the countess to court. Of course, they didn't actually leave the King's Seat, as the countess's quarters and the various rooms and halls where the court's events happened were all in the Seat.

They entered the throne room for the first happening of the day. The regent was holding court. The countess had explained that the prince regent was lax in his official court duties. He would hold court for a few hours in the morning, then a short time after lunch, and then be about his own entertainment: hawking, hunting, or other sport. She explained that the old king had held court each day until the daily business was done, usually without a deadline.

The countess and Twee were announced. Of course, the twenty guardsmen, ladies-in-waiting, and other servants in their retinue weren't.

"Her ladyship, the countess Olivia D'Arilo and her nephew Twilight D'Arilo," the court marshal announced. He had a similar tone and vocal quality to how the countess's gentleman usher announced her arrival in Twee's cell an eternity ago. *They must train their voices somewhere*, Twee thought.

The countess explained to Twee that a nephew visiting from D'Arilo should be a good cover, seeing as most people at court would have no idea who he was.

"But," Twee asked, "if the regent and his people know who I am, why won't they just grab me?"

"There are a couple of reasons why I'm hoping we don't have to worry about that," the countess explained. "The regent is not popular, and his unpopularity's core is his conflict with the concept of law. It would be a very unpopular move for him to flaunt the law by such an illegal act, especially in such a public place as the court."

"Also," she continued with a wink, "His chief minister, who you will meet or, at least, see in court, is sympathetic to our cause. He's got the regent's ear and has convinced him such an act would be unwise."

"What is our cause?" said Twee.

"All in good time, my dear. Don't forget, you are my younger brother's middle son from his second marriage." said the countess.

Court had not yet started. This was still when the various courtiers, nobles, and other court attendees arrived and took up their positions.

They were in the same chamber where the prince regent had interviewed Twee. The countess, Twee, and their retinue took position on the side of the room under one of the high windows lining the walls. The countess tried to get them close to the throne.

"Normally," she whispered to Twee, "I wouldn't care, but I want the regent to see you. I want to see his reaction."

The regent wasn't there yet. The countess explained he didn't arrive until after the rest of the court was in position. He had a strong feeling his time was more important than theirs.

More courtiers, nobles, and their retinues arrived. The court marshal announced each group. Twee tried to keep track of the names and titles of the arrivals. The countess tried to fill him in on the people already present, but there were so many. The labels seemed so meaningless to him.

One who was announced as "Lord Taedum" was more important. The countess pointed him out among his retinue. He was the chief minister. The one who had the regent's ear but was sympathetic to "our cause."

Even though he was taller than the members of his retinue, he was somehow still hard to pick out of the crowd. He had blond hair, like the countess. Her hair color reminded Twee of the sun glowing on a haystack on a summer day. Lord Taedum's made Twee think of the color of an unripe kernel of corn after it had been trodden on by a mule.

As he walked by the spot where the countess and Twee were, his bright eyes, which looked vaguely predatory to Twee, swept over them and came to rest on Twee. Twee stood a little straighter.

Lord Taedum took up a position just to the side of the throne.

The Young Lion arrived.

"His highness, Liam Aimar, the prince regent."

"Lord Cole Aimar was Liam's father," the countess whispered to Twee. "A Liamec noble from the south of the country. No one special, really. Which is part of the prince regent's problem."

As the regent and his retinue strode down the scarlet carpet toward the throne and its supporting dais, Twee observed again how majestic he was. Some of the crowd standing near Twee and the countess noticed as well. Twee heard giggles from some young women standing not far from them.

As the regent drew near to their position, Twee felt his gaze. He felt the urge to step backward and disappear into the countess's shadow, but he didn't. Twee stood his ground again. He had heard the expression "if looks could kill" a few times in the outlaw camp and later in Grisput. He never really understood what it meant until now.

The court and the rest of the day were anticlimactic after the preliminaries. The Young Lion settled back on his throne and seemed bored.

The court of the King's Bench, which this was, was the highest court in the kingdom. Cases were brought here if they were left undecided in lower courts or challenged. The rationale was that the king was a higher power, and his wisdom would illuminate the case's murkiness.

Therefore, the cases were complex and controversial. The Young Lion might have been interested in the controversy, but he couldn't be bothered with the complexity. He mostly left the decisions to the chief minister and his other advisers.

Occasionally he showed more interest. It often seemed his advisers were spending most of their time trying to talk him out of things when he did. A couple of times, he got pretty insistent about something. Once after one of these moments, Twee caught an expression of distaste on Lord Taedum's face.

The lunch break was worse. The countess took Twee around and introduced him to an interminable list of nobles, courtiers, and other dignitaries. Twee went through the motions but found himself losing interest more and more quickly with each introduction.

The afternoon session was more of the same, and Twee felt an unwelcome sympathy with the Young Lion's boredom.

Twee was relieved to return to the Ruby wing at the end of the day.

# 12

Twee tried to clean Vix up that evening. They had a water basin from the privy nook that was warm earlier. By the time Vix came by his room, it was cold. Vix didn't mind. She was used to washing in cold water when she washed at all.

Twee tried to get Vix clean, but she resisted. Not actively, but in a passive way, by not helping him much. He managed to get a lot of soot and grime off her face and some off her arms and legs, but he really had no idea what to do with her hair. It was quite a bit longer than when he first met her. Now the tangled hair dangled down to her shoulders. In color, it was a mix of copper-red and black and gray from whatever muck was mixed into it.

Twee had a hairbrush left by the washbasin in the privy nook. He didn't know how to use it on himself, and he didn't really need to. Fortunately for him, the current hair fashion in court for young men was short hair.

The hairbrush got stuck when Twee tried to run it through Vix's hair. He tried several times, and each time, it held so fast that it was not very easy to get out. Eventually, he gave up. He had what he thought was a brilliant solution. He decided he would tuck her hair into a cap.

Twee didn't have any clothes for Vix, except for the ones they had given him. They were big on her, but they managed to get her into a pair of britches and a tunic.

"Vix," said Twee, glancing at her burlap smock, "you should take the stuff out of the pockets. If they find it, they'll burn it, and I don't know what they'll think of your stuff."

Twee helped Vix find a place to put her pockets' contents. There were several dressers in his room, and he didn't have anything in them other than the clothes they had made for him.

Vix and Twee cleaned out one of the drawers, and Vix put her things in it.

Twee didn't know where to look while Vix was unloading her pockets. He was curious about the contents, but watching her empty them was somehow more of an invasion of her privacy than helping her dress was. He glimpsed the bottle of Mama's spit, which she used to heal his clipped ear, and something which looked like a folded-up pile of cobwebs before he turned away.

When they were done, Twee inspected the result. Vix was still a little shorter than him, and she had a tendency to slouch a little, so she looked even smaller. She was dressed in boy's clothes, too big for her, so the sleeve ends dangled below her hands, and the ankle cuffs were dragging on the ground. Her hair was tucked into the cap she wore, though sooty copper strands were trailing out from all sides.

Twee's shoes didn't fit her. Her feet were the consistency of boiled leather, and they were black with grime on both the bottoms and the sides. Twee tried to scrub them a little, but the color didn't change.

But she was clean. Or at least cleaner than she was. Also, a somewhat fresher smell had replaced the odor of moldy burlap.

Twee felt he had accomplished a monumental feat and looked forward to introducing Vix to the countess in the morning.

# 13

They located the countess at breakfast in her breakfast nook. The nook was actually a room in a high tower that rose over the Ruby wing. It had a spectacular view of the King's Seat spread out below. The first time Twee saw the Seat from the breakfast nook windows, he stood by the window and stared out at it for what felt like hours.

You could see nothing but castle walls, towers, battlements, and more conventional-looking rooftops, spread out below as far as the eye could see. It was certainly possible that the regent was impoverishing the kingdom by building the Seat, as many complained, but it was nothing short of spectacular.

As Twee and Vix walked through the wing corridors trying to locate the countess, they were greeted and challenged, amicably, by several guardsmen. The guardsmen had come to know Twee and knew he had the run of the wing.

Twee disarmed them by asking where the countess was and explaining that Vix was his cousin, who he wanted to introduce to her. Aside from a few skeptical looks, this explanation was enough to get by.

As the two entered the breakfast nook, the countess's gentleman usher began to announce them, but the countess waved him to silence. Twee wondered when the man took time for himself. He seemed to always be present at the door of whatever room the countess was in.

Twee and Vix made their way over to the countess.

"Now, who is this?" said the countess.

Vix attempted the curtsy that Twee had tried to teach her last night. The ankle cuffs on her pants were dragging on the floor, so the gesture didn't come off as well as it might have.

In fact, she almost wound up falling down, but she managed to avoid that ignominious fate. The curtsy didn't look as polished as it should.

"Her name is Vix," said Twee. "She followed me from Grisput."

"Well, that was very enterprising," said the countess. She rose and walked over to Vix. Putting her hand under Vix's chin, she lifted her head and turned her face to one side and then the other.

"This is a girl?" she asked. Twee was silent. He was just relieved Vix hadn't tried to bite the countess's hand.

"This will never do," said the countess. "Agnes!" she called.

Agnes arrived, and as she had with Twee, she bundled Vix off for treatment. Twee tried to reassure her with a calming touch on her shoulder as she left, but he could see the worry in her eyes.

The countess and Twee retired to the drawing-room for a discussion.

"Now, who is this?" repeated the countess.

"Your ladyship," said Twee, "I was hoping you could help her like you helped me. She's a very dear friend who I know from Grisput."

"I'm sure something can be done," the countess said. "There are still empty rooms in the Ruby wing."

Twee and the countess fell silent for a while. They waited for what seemed to Twee like an eternity.

There was a knock on the door. After a brief whispered consultation between the gentleman usher and Agnes, the usher called out, "The Lady Vix."

Twee rose to his feet as Vix walked into the room. Agnes and her working crew had engineered a miracle in almost no time.

Twee was stunned. He didn't recognize this person walking toward him, but she was the most beautiful young woman he had ever seen. She wore an evening gown of green silk, though it was still before noon. The green dress offset the copper hues of her hair, which shone like a bright, shiny new copper coin and looked clean through some further miracle.

The gown flowed down her body and showed she actually had a shape, and quite a nice shape, which the burlap had wholly concealed.

Twee felt his breathing hasten. Back in Grisput, women in the craftsman's district had sometimes approached him, but he had been unsure of himself and out of his depth. He felt the same way now, but the urge to figure out how to overcome the sensation was new.

Vix stepped toward him. The countess was watching this interaction with amusement. Vix stepped forward again. Her feet tangled in the hem of the gown, or perhaps under it, as she wore unfamiliar shoes. She tripped and fell toward Twee. Twee noticed for the first time that there were tears in her eyes.

Twee caught her, and her head fell against his shoulder. Without any hint of moldy burlap, the smell of soap and Vix reached him. Vix started sobbing like her heart was breaking.

"Twee," she sobbed, "it has no pockets."

# LION

# 1

The countess insisted Vix join Twee in the lessons she was having him take. In addition to ordinary things, like reading, writing, and arithmetic, they got sessions on history and etiquette. Twee wasn't sure what the point of the etiquette lessons was, but he enjoyed history.

At one point, their tutor discussed the kings of Liamec. He described the reign of Liam III, or the old king, as many referred to him these days.

"In his heyday, Liam III got a great deal of attention for his reformation of the legal system of Liamec," the tutor intoned. "This was positive attention from many, though the older nobles and aristocrats were concerned about what it meant to their power and authority."

"Isn't Liam III still king?" said Twee.

The tutor looked a little disturbed at being interrupted but perhaps pleased at this sign that Twee was listening.

"In a sense. For the last ten years, since the king's council declared the old king infirm, the prince regent has been administering the kingdom."

"When the old king dies, who will be king?" said Vix.

The tutor blinked and sat for a moment in silence. Vix wasn't used to being in the lessons, and she lowered her head, thinking she had said something wrong.

"That's a good question, Vix," the tutor said seriously. Vix looked back up. "Without an easy answer."

He paused again as if thinking about what to say next.

"They declared the old king infirm before he could name an heir. He had two children. A son and a daughter."

Again the tutor paused. As if he was trying to pick his way through the verbal equivalent of a field strewn with hidden bear traps.

"The son, Liam, disappeared about twenty-five years before the council declared Liam III infirm. In the normal course of events, he would be the heir."

He continued in something approaching a whisper, "Or his male offspring.

"No one knows exactly what happened to Liam, who would have been Liam IV. There were crazy stories that he abdicated and left his royal duties to become a farmer. They tried to get the Academy mages to track him down, but something blocked their attempts. They could verify he was still alive but could not find out where he was."

The tutor took a breath and continued, "Liam III's daughter, Linota, didn't have any male offspring. Her eldest daughter, Louisa, married a noble from the southern part of Liamec, Cole Aimar. Their eldest son, Liam Aimar, is our prince regent."

"So, the prince regent has the best claim to the throne," said Vix.

"If there are any male descendants of the old king's son Liam still alive, they have a much stronger claim," said the tutor. Again his voice lowered as he said this, though they were the only ones in the room. "Our traditions and laws are unambiguous on male inheritance. Both the countess and the prince regent are not fond of this for very different reasons, but that's how it is.

"If the prince regent's father, or his grandfather, had been a descendant of Liam III, he would already be king."

## 2

Twee and Vix accompanied the countess to court. The clothes Vix had been given were appropriate for a lady-in-waiting. The countess thought a second out-of-town relative might raise suspicions about the first. Vix walked a step behind with the retinue as they entered.

Vix had convinced Agnes to make some unique clothes for her for regular wear. The first clothes Vix had gotten made her feel that she couldn't do anything other than stand around in them. They compromised on a riding outfit, the thing Vix liked best among the options. She persuaded them to add pockets, and Twee knew she had gotten hold of a needle and thread and added additional hidden pockets herself.

The countess frowned whenever she saw Vix wearing this outfit, and Vix would try to hide if she saw Agnes coming down a corridor. Twee thought it looked fetching.

For the court, they denied it. She wore a lady-in-waiting dress. Twee could see her fidgeting and patting her sides, searching for the missing pockets.

Once they got into their position on the side of the room, Twee and Vix could stand side by side. Twee watched while Vix took in the sights and observed the introductions. She gave a hint of a gasp when the prince regent was introduced. The Lion's presence had struck Twee similarly when he first saw him, but he couldn't help but feel a surge of jealousy when he saw Vix react the same way.

The court session was similar to last time. The regent looked bored. The issues and cases presented were involved, but they didn't absorb either the regent's or Twee's attention. Then, after the court had been in session for an hour, Twee saw the regent sit up and start to focus. He leaned over to Lord Taedum, the chief minister, and asked him something. After hearing the minister's response, the regent stood and stepped to the front of the dais. Abruptly, his whole attention focused on the main door to the throne room at the opposite end of the crimson carpet.

Two of the king's guardsmen entered. Their blue tabarded uniforms with the black silhouette of the lion's head still gave Twee a momentary chill. Twee recognized the position and pose from when they had dragged him through the castle. They were holding a man between them.

The man's arms were shackled behind himself. The two guardsmen each had a hand on one of his shoulders. He wasn't a tall man, but he held himself well. He had a little blood trickling down from one side of his mouth and a black and blue eye. It didn't look like the guardsmen were treating him particularly well. His hair was jet black, and though he might be old enough for it to gray, his hair, either out of respect or fear, maintained the inky blackness.

The guardsmen pulled him forward until they reached the foot of the dais. The Young Lion was practically bursting with excitement for the first time that day. Twee recognized the scene. Except for the different people present, everything was similar to when he had been brought before the regent.

The guardsmen threw the prisoner to the floor, forcing him to kneel. The regent stepped down the stairs, stopping on the last step above where the man knelt. Kneeling made the prisoner even smaller.

"This little man," said the regent. "This little man is the one who's been giving my troops and tax collectors so much trouble?"

The regent spat on the top of the man's head below him. He turned to the crowd.

"Ladies and gentlemen," he announced proudly. "I give you: The mighty Raven!"

## 3

Twee gasped. Loud enough that the surrounding people turned to look at him. Vix looked at him as well, with a curious expression on her face. In their years of breaking bread together, they had both carefully avoided talking about or asking about their pasts.

Twee looked around himself at the reactions of the others in the crowd. Most everyone seemed shocked. There was an excited murmur rippling like a wave through them. There were several people, however, who looked less surprised. One man standing not far from Twee, part of another noble's retinue, nodded.

Twee moved over next to him and, as casually as he could manage, asked, "What about the rest of them? The rest of the Raven's men? The other outlaws?"

The man, seeming a little annoyed at having his attention drawn away from the spectacle, said, "Who cares? He was the ringleader."

Twee insisted, "But weren't others captured? Did they kill them all?"

"I think I heard that others were in the dungeon," the man said. "But, really, what does it matter? They'll hang them all, anyway." He looked at Twee a little curiously.

Twee stepped back to his place beside Vix. He turned again to look at what was happening before the throne.

The Lion drew the Raven to his feet. He towered over the shorter man, partly because he was taller and partly because he was still standing on the first of the dais steps.

"This little man has caused me so much trouble," said the regent. He pulled a dagger from his belt. Weapons were forbidden in the throne room while the court of the king's bench was in session except for the guardsmen. It seemed the regent could bend that rule.

The regent laid the dagger against the Raven's throat. The Raven didn't flinch. He stood stoically, waiting for whatever came.

"I should kill you now. Right here in front of all these people."

Twee tensed. There was nothing he could do, but at the same time, he felt he had to do something. If the regent had killed the Raven, he probably would have charged forward toward him.

Vix looked at Twee oddly. It was clear she could see the tension in his body.

The regent pulled the dagger away from the Raven's throat.

"But I have a better idea," he said theatrically. Twee got the impression the threat was scripted.

"You and your surviving crew of outlaws will rot in jail for one hour for each gold coin you took from me."

The expression on the Lion's face got darker and more vicious with each word.

"On the day of the midsummer festival, we will hang you and your band of villains at the height of the festivities."

This idea seemed to please the Lion, and he smiled as he continued, "People will bring their families and make it an outing. They will see what happens to those who stand against me and know that I am the strongest."

# 4

Later, when they were alone, Twee broke the unwritten rule about not talking about their pasts and spoke to Vix about his time in the outlaw camp. He didn't go so far as to tell her about his life before the outlaws, with the wolves. As he spoke about Anne, Bear, Oscar, and Jordan and looked into her green eyes, he realized she was the one who would hear that story as well.

Vix looked torn. Twee breaking the rule had changed something.

"My mother was one of the cunning folk," she said. Twee remembered what Oscar had told him about the cunning folk, the mages from the Academy, the hedgewitches, and the three magic types.

"She was the cunning woman of a little village near Grisput," Vix continued. "The bond market must have been low on merchandise that year or something because the Grisput guard raided the village and took everyone prisoner. Trumped-up charges, I guess. They said everyone had a bond debt to pay.

"They let my mother keep me because I was too young to be much use for anything."

Vix looked down at the ground, and Twee put his hand on her shoulder.

"She didn't last very long," she breathed. "I managed to get away before they could catch me.

"I guess my mother didn't take well to being a bondy," Vix concluded.

Vix took Twee to a place in the Emerald wing. They now had permission from the countess to freely roam the Ruby and Emerald wings. The Ruby wing was where the countess and most of her attendants lived. The Emerald wing was mainly for the use of her guard.

They were in an empty, unused room overlooking a courtyard. Of course, the yard didn't lead out of the King's Seat, as with everything else within quite a distance. But it was adjacent to one of the castle dungeons, and the king's guards used it as an exercise yard for prisoners.

Vix had worked out when they were bringing prisoners out to get air. The guardsmen really had no strong desire to treat their prisoners well enough to give them air or exercise. But it was one of the legal reforms implemented by the old king Liam III during his reformation. The prince regent hadn't figured out a way to eliminate it yet.

Twee and Vix looked out the window at the yard below. It was far enough that there was no way to make out faces, but you could see the blue tabards on the king's guardsmen. They hoped they might make out enough to learn something.

A line of prisoners was led out into the open space through a wooden door. The guards pulled them roughly into the yard. Twee and Vix could make out the sound of the guards calling to each other.

There were eight figures in the line.

Tears came to Twee's eyes. He turned his back to the window and slumped to the ground.

Vix knelt beside him. "Twee," she said. "What's wrong? Are you all right?"

"I think that's Anne," Twee sobbed, "in the blue. At the back." He wiped his eyes, stood, and looked out the window again.

"And that might be Bear," he said, "the big one, in the middle."

# 5

There was a knock on Twee's door in the middle of the night. Since they'd been able to see each other during the day, Vix hadn't been coming to visit in the evenings, so Twee wasn't sure what it was.

It was Vix. She stood fully dressed in the corridor, in her riding outfit. Twee pulled her inside and shut the door. He was wearing his nightshirt.

"Get dressed, Twee," said Vix. "I have something to show you."

Twee got some clothes out of his dresser. Vix just waited patiently. She looked at him with curiosity, waiting for him to get dressed.

Twee began to pull off his nightshirt, then he flushed slightly, bundled up his clothes, and stepped behind the screen in the privy nook.

Twee dressed quickly in the nook's privacy and followed Vix out the door into the corridor.

It was late, and Twee wasn't sure what the guards would think, seeing the two of them wandering around in the halls at night. Apparently, Vix had the same thought. She dug around in her outfit's pockets and pulled out a folded-up piece of ratty old cloth. It looked like it was covered with cobwebs, or perhaps it was made out of cobwebs.

Vix unfolded the piece of fabric and started spreading it out.

"You'll have to stand close to me," she said. "I didn't mean it to be big enough for two."

Vix spread the cloth over her head. The places where fabric covered her became almost impossible to see. It was as if the material looked like whatever was behind it, more than like itself. Vix lifted up one corner of the cloth and whispered to Twee, “Get under here.”

Now Twee understood how Vix knew so much about the castle corridor layout and how she made her way to his cell when he first got to Capitol. It still didn’t explain how she got from Grisput to Capitol herself, but that was a question for another time.

He squeezed under the cloth. It really wasn’t big enough for two. He had to press tightly up against Vix to allow both of them to fit. He was a little taller than Vix, so he found himself with his face directly above her head. He took in the smell of her hair and the feeling of being close to her. The scent of Vix’s hair mixed with the moldy, cobwebby smell of the cloth they had draped over their heads.

Vix set off urgently down the corridor, and Twee had to shuffle awkwardly after her to keep up and keep under the fabric.

Around the next bend, a guard walked down the center of the corridor in their direction. In a practiced fashion, made a little more complicated by Twee’s presence, Vix stepped to the side and froze while the guard walked past.

After he passed, Twee whispered to Vix, “What is this thing?”

Vix shushed him and whispered urgently, “My mother taught me how to make it.”

It seemed to Twee that they walked through interminable corridors. Vix knew every turn. They started by heading through the ruby wing to the emerald wing, then continued. The trip was made less painful for Twee by his pleasure at standing so close to Vix. When there weren’t any guards around, they could maintain a little distance. Each time a guard came near, they squeezed closer together to remain hidden under the cloth.

They left the emerald wing. Twee noticed a clear border where the countess’s domain ended, guarded by her guardsmen in their yellow bird of prey tabards.

Vix led Twee downward into the depths, out of the castle's upper levels. The stone walls of the corridors down here weren't kept clean or decorated with tapestries. In spots, there was mold growing on the walls.

They approached a guard station and had to squeeze together and creep awkwardly past. The room beyond was empty but had some unfinished wooden furniture. Vix grabbed a short wooden stool and brought it under the cloth with them.

"What's that for?" Twee whispered.

"You'll see," said Vix.

Beyond that room was a corridor with a row of locked doors that were clearly cells. Vix had brought them to one of the castle dungeons. She stopped at one door and put the stool down on the floor. Vix pointed to the high iron-barred window. Twee stepped up on the stool. The corridor was dimly lit by torchlight, but the cell beyond was pitch black.

"It's dark. I can't see anything," Twee whispered. Vix hopped up onto the stool next to him. He kept his balance by putting his hand on the wall. The stool's top wasn't very wide, so Vix had to squeeze tight to Twee to stand there. She pulled something out of one of her pockets. It looked like a wad of spiderwebs and dust. She pulled a pinch of whatever it was off the clump and dabbed it into Twee's eyes. It stung, and he blinked.

Vix jumped back down off the stool. Twee blinked a little more until his vision cleared. He looked again through the bars into the dark cell. Things seemed brighter. Now he could see through the gloom to a pallet on the other side. A man lay on the rough bed facing toward the door.

It was Bear.

# 6

It was still dark, and even with Vix's webs in his eyes, Twee couldn't see Bear clearly. From what he could see, Bear didn't look very good. His clothes were dirty and blood-stained, and his face looked rough and beaten. But it was Bear. Twee was elated and worried at the same time. He had never imagined seeing his old companions from the outlaw camp again. But he worried about what the regent had said about the midsummer festival.

"Bear," Twee whispered urgently. He tried to make his voice carry into the cell without it carrying down the corridor. The guards weren't that far away.

There was no response from the sleeping man. Twee could hear Bear's heavy breathing; it didn't sound healthy.

"Bear!" Twee whispered again, trying to be a little louder this time. Bear's breathing caught, and he groaned. He shifted on the pallet, and the labored breathing turned into labored snoring.

"Bear!" Twee called this time, desperate to get Bear's attention. Below him, he saw Vix look down the corridor in the direction of the guardroom. Bear grunted and sat up partway on the pallet.

"Is someone there?" he said.

"Bear," Twee whispered, "it's me, Twee."

"Twee?" said Bear. He looked confused. He also looked like just sitting up had caused him pain.

"Twee?" repeated Bear, and he began to cry.

"Bear?" said Twee, "it's all right. I'm here to help."

"I've had this dream before, Twee," said Bear slowly and carefully. "Since we let you down in the forest, I've dreamed this many times."

"It's not a dream, Bear. I'm really here," Twee said. Twee worried. Bear still sounded confused. As he blinked the spiderwebs deeper into his eyes and his vision cleared more, he could see beads of sweat on Bear's forehead.

Twee turned to Vix and said, "Vix, do you still have your bottle of 'Mother's Tears'? The one you used to fix my ear?"

"'Mama's Spit,'" said Vix. She pulled the little bottle out of a pocket.

Twee reached down and took the bottle from Vix's hand. He made a throwing gesture and looked at her. She nodded.

Twee turned back to the window and tried to figure out the best way to throw the bottle to Bear.

"Bear," he said, "I'm going to throw something to you. Don't try to catch it. I know you can't see much. I'll throw it, then tell you where it landed."

"Twee," said Bear, "I'm so sorry. We looked for you, and when we didn't find a body, we hoped, but we had no way to know if or where they took you."

Twee threw the bottle. It was a good throw. It bounced off of Bear's stomach and clattered to the floor below the pallet. It didn't sound like it broke.

"Feel around for the bottle, Bear," said Twee. "It's a healing thing. Put a drop on each of your wounds. It might sting, but it should help."

There were shuffling noises as Bear reached below the pallet and found the bottle. He groaned a little each time he moved. As Bear found the bottle, picked it up, and started dabbing drops on his injuries, Twee continued, "How about the others, Bear? Who's here? What happened?"

Bear groaned again softly before he replied. Twee imagined the "Mama's Spit" probably stung much worse on his deeper wounds than it had on Twee's clipped ear.

"It must have been an inside job," said Bear. "They knew right where to find us. Someone must have told them something." He sighed. "There were so many of them, and they surprised us. I didn't see what happened to Oscar. I hope he got away. He was always a tricky one."

"Anne's here," Bear continued.

Twee breathed a sigh of relief. He hadn't been fooling himself with his sighting of the spot of blue in the exercise yard.

"I'm sorry, Twee," said Bear. "Jordan didn't make it. It was amazing how well he did with that little pig-sticker of his," Bear continued sadly, "but there were just too many."

Vix tugged at Twee's shirt urgently. Sounds were coming from down the corridor.

"Arturo," said Twee, "I've got to go. Tell the others. I'll get you out."

# 7

The countess introduced her "nephew" to many nobles, aristocrats, and other influential people of the court and government. Each time, there was some polite conversation, and Twee would get to exercise his etiquette lessons. Then something would happen, or the countess would suggest something to Twee, and he could escape.

After a while, he started to suspect this wasn't just something the countess was arranging to allow him to leave the conversations before his etiquette lessons failed. Instead, there might be some other motive for her to get him to go. He observed that the conversations often got more intimate and intense when he was no longer part of them.

He also noticed the countess was introducing him around quite a lot. When they attended court, at dinner parties, and on other occasions. He recognized a few other things as well. After these conversations, the people the countess talked with would treat him differently. They were careful when talking to him. They would address him very formally and appeared to avoid some topics of conversation.

At first, he thought they were just polite, or perhaps the countess had warned them he was new to the court, then he started to suspect there was more to it.

Vix assured Twee she would watch the Raven's men in the dungeons.

"The countess keeps you so busy," she said, "and I have lots of time while you're attending court or going to dinner parties as her nephew."

Twee wanted to see the prisoners again, especially Anne, but Vix told him, "The women's ward is more secure. It's too dangerous."

Vix kept track of what happened to the prisoners. She watched them in the prison yard.

"Bear seems to be moving much better. Anne is very pretty for an old lady, isn't she?"

The countess and Twee were at a dinner party for Lord Beaumont, the Warden of the Blue Mountains. Before arriving, Twee was briefed on Lord Beaumont's rank and status.

"The title is a bit of a misnomer. Lord Beaumont is not really in charge of the blue mountains. His province extends from the ocean in the north, about halfway down the eastern border of Liamec. South of his lands is a group of independent towns and villages called the Crossroads. But his lands are very extensive in that part of the country."

"His lands and armies," continued the countess, "are a significant part of the state of Liamec, and he is a force to be reckoned with in court politics."

Before dinner, the party met in the Lord's hall. Twee was introduced to Lord Beaumont, and then, as usual, the countess gave him a pretext to leave. Usually, he would have wandered off to meet and greet with other guests, but on this occasion, he worked his way back to get close enough to the countess and the Lord to hear part of what was said.

Their voices turned quiet when just the two of them spoke, and Twee couldn't hear every word. The fragments of the conversation which he picked up were intriguing, however.

"It's positive," Twee heard the countess say. "The bloodline has been confirmed."

"If that's true," said Lord Beaumont. "You can count me in."

After Twee returned from one of these events, he asked Vix if she had learned anything about the prisoners.

"They're all right," said Vix, "as well as can be expected."

"It's only two months until the midsummer festival," said

Twee, "I need to figure out what to do."

# 8

The countess summoned Twee to her drawing-room. "Lord Twilight," the gentleman usher announced. The countess was sitting at a small table and gestured Twee over. She motioned for him to sit in a seat opposite her.

"Twee," she said, "you're a smart young man, and you've probably figured most of this out yourself, but I think it's time to lay our cards on the table."

Twee looked for the deck. She had been teaching him to play bridge.

"Let me quote more of the prophecy the academy clairvoyant delivered."

The countess paused and drew a breath.

"Twilight shall come, and the young lion will fall in the darkness. The lion will fall, and the wolf will rise."

Twee frowned. He wasn't sure he liked where this was going.

"The land will join around him, and twilight will shine a light into the night.

"The son of the son of the old lion who has his heart, he who turns night into day, and day into night, will light this land into a new dawn.

"It goes on like that," said the countess. "It gets to be a bit much after a while, but it does paint you in a good light if you read it that way."

"Me?" said Twee.

The countess looked at Twee, arching an eyebrow. "Surely you realize this is about you. I already told you the prophecy was about you. You haven't wondered why the prince regent stares at you in court? Or why he arrested you in the first place?"

"I've been trying not to think about it," said Twee.

"The time will come when you will have to grasp your destiny, Twee," said the countess. "And it may come sooner than we think. You are the grandson of the son of the old king. I knew your grandfather when we were both young. I never met your father, he may not even know who he is, but you need to know who you are. We're waiting for the regent to make the first move, but his impatience is building, and I'm sure it won't be long now."

"But, how do you know for sure?" said Twee. He was desperate to figure out some way to believe this wasn't true.

"I've had it confirmed multiple times by alchemists from the Academy. You are who you are. And, while perhaps it shouldn't, it means a great deal."

Later, when they were alone together, Vix rubbed Twee's shoulder.

"It's not the worst thing in the world," she said. "Maybe you can do some good things."

Twee looked at her. He felt trapped. In some ways, this felt like a trap closing around him tighter than the bond market in Grisput.

"Remember the old king and all the good things the tutor told us he did?"

Vix continued, "Strengthening laws, punishing crimes, freeing people who have been unjustly imprisoned, and other things like that. Maybe you could be the next good king?"

Twee perked up a bit at that idea. "Maybe I could do something about the bond market in Grisput."

"Maybe you could," said Vix.

"I could free Anne, Bear, and the Raven," said Twee, with sudden determination.

# 9

The old king died. As far as anyone knew, it was from natural causes. The story whispered around the King's Seat before the official news came out was that he had just not woken up one morning and was found peacefully in his bed.

Twee regretted never meeting him. He had been sequestered in his sickbed for years, and the countess hadn't considered it relevant. From what she told Twee about his parentage, he knew the old king was supposed to be his great grandfather. Twee had never had a real family, except for Misha, and would have liked to have met him before he died.

There was a state funeral. The procession from the King's Seat to the royal cemetery was the first time Twee had been outside the Seat since his arrival. Even the arms training and riding lessons Twee and Vix took were in courtyards, gardens, and tracks within the Seat.

Vix and Twee traveled as part of the countess's retinue in the procession. The procession wound from the massive First Courtyard of the Seat through the Noble Quarter to the royal cemetery on a hill overlooking the quarter.

As the carriage they were riding in climbed the hill to the cemetery, Twee turned to look out over the Noble Quarter and the King's Seat. The Noble Quarter had walls that separated the quarter from the rest of Capitol. Twee marveled at the view. The Seat was spread out below. To Twee, the Seat looked as big as all of Grisput.

The prince regent didn't attend the funeral. It was a bit of a scandal. Twee overheard snatches of conversation where people muttered about that at the funeral and later at the reception.

At the reception, the countess was very busy. She was eager to touch base with each of the nobles and dignitaries there. She didn't ask Twee to meet anyone this time around, so he and Vix snuck away to a private corner to talk.

"Twee," said Vix, "You've got to be careful." She looked at him thoughtfully. "I heard some people talking. They say this may be the moment the regent is waiting for.

"The old king dying means the prince regent isn't regent for anyone specific anymore. He will pick this moment to declare himself king. It won't be legal, so he'll have to work around the law."

When the countess's retinue returned from the funeral, the yellow tabarded guardsmen seemed particularly watchful. As they passed through the Emerald wing on their way to the Ruby wing, Twee noticed a great deal of activity. More guardsmen moved about the corridors, and there was more going on than usual.

# 10

Twee awoke early to noises in the corridor outside his room. He dressed quickly, making sure to wear his boots with the concealed sheath and slip his tooth into it. He went to the door.

He listened before opening the door. Two voices were murmuring. He wasn't sure what noise had woken him, but there weren't usually people posted there, so something was up.

There were two guards outside. One was stationed on each side of the door frame. They were wearing the yellow tabard with the grasping raptor claw of the countess's guardsmen.

One of the guardsmen turned to Twee as he opened the door.

"Your Majesty," he said.

"What did you call me?" said Twee.

"Lord Twilight," the man corrected himself, "we need you to stay inside, on the countess's orders."

"I need to see what's going on," said Twee. He started to step out of the doorway.

The guardsman lowered his spear across Twee's path.

"I'm afraid I must insist, my lord," he said.

"What is this?" said Twee.

"We're under orders from the countess to keep you safe," said the guardsman. "Please go back inside and bar the door."

There was a bar inside the door, which Twee had never used. Clearly, the guards weren't going to budge, so Twee closed the door and put the bar in place.

He went to the window and looked out onto the courtyard below. It was between the Ruby wing and the Sapphire wing. There wasn't usually much going on in this courtyard, and

Twee's window was high above it. Typically, he would see one or two of the countess's guardsmen below, going about their business, and sometimes one of the blue tabarded king's men. Today, in contrast, there was a crowd of the countess's men in their yellow and none of the king's men. The guardsmen he could see were preparing for something.

Twee watched for a while. He could see visible urgency in the guard's movements, but there wasn't much he could pick out about what was going on from his height. He could hear their voices when they spoke loudly or yelled but couldn't understand the specifics.

Twee began to get very frustrated. In Grisput, as a bondy, he learned to swallow his anger and pride. Since coming to Capitol with the countess's lessons and training, he had started expecting his life to have a little more agency.

He left the window and began pacing back and forth across the room. The feeling of helplessness was overpowering. He thought about opening the door again, but the guards had made their orders clear, and he was sure the result would be the same.

Some sounds came from the window. Twee raced back to the windowsill and looked down again. The scene below was one of chaos. The courtyard was filled with men in the regent's blue tabards and the countess's guards trying to hold them back. The sounds of the struggle were loud enough to reach his window, including the cries of pain when a blow struck.

Twee took in the scene below, then ran back to the door. He needed to get out and find a way to help, though where he should go and what he should do were still unclear.

Sounds were coming from the hallway, as well. Twee heard the distinct sound of metal on metal and then a cry of pain. There was a banging on the door.

Twee pulled the bar out of the door. Maybe the guards outside needed help.

The door burst open as someone kicked it from the

outside. An armored guardsman in the blue tabard of the king's men burst in, sword in hand.

# 11

Twee took in the scene in the hall in a flash. The two guardsmen he had spoken with earlier were lying in crumpled heaps on the floor. There was another guardsman in blue slumped against the far wall of the corridor.

Twee smelled the acrid scent of smoke in the air. There must be a fire burning somewhere. Most of the King's Seat was stone, but there was enough wood that fire was a real danger.

Twee didn't have time to think about anything that far away as the guardsman charging into the room swung his sword in a sweeping blow towards his head.

Twee thought that perhaps the man might have been better off with a thrust as he dropped to the ground, rolled under the blow, and pulled his tooth out of his boot sheath in a single movement.

*A thrust*, Twee thought, as he rose to his feet and faced his opponent, *is a faster motion and harder to dodge.*

Twee crouched in a knife fighter's ready stance. His years of training with Jordan, Bear, and, more recently, the countess's master of arms filled his head. Bear had emphasized the sword and spear, but while Jordan preferred the knife on knife duels, he had spent quite a bit of time on mismatched fights.

"In a battle," Jordan had said, "You can't control how your opponent is armed or armored."

The guardsman looked at Twee. He had a grizzled face. A scar ran from the left side of his cheek, through his lip, and across to below his nose. It made his face look sinister.

Then, abruptly, the guardsman smiled. The smile cracked the scar line across his mouth and made him look friendly and pleasant for a moment. He readied his sword for another swing.

Twee smiled as well. He hoped the guardsman's superior

weapon, armor, and strength would make him overconfident. Twee needed an edge of any kind.

The guardsman began another strike with his sword. Twee prepared to dive under the swing again, then something about how the man moved made him change his maneuver.

Instead of rolling under the swing, Twee darted back out of reach of the man's sword. The guardsman didn't have time to change his move. He halted the left-to-right motion halfway through the swing and plummeted his sword straight down. The sword blow might have reached him if Twee had dropped and rolled as he had on the first swing.

The guardsman's breathing was a little labored. He had already had to battle with the countess's men out in the hall. Twee was still fresh.

The man took another swing. Twee ducked and rolled again. This time, he dove under the blow and toward the guardsman. He steered his rolling body into the man's leg, staggering him and leaving Twee within the guardsman's reach but close enough that the sword was unwieldy. Twee smelled the sour smell of the man's sweat. Regaining his feet, he stabbed upward with his tooth with all his might. The knife caught in one link of the guard's chain-mail. Probably causing a nasty bruise, but not any serious injury.

Twee scrambled to get out of the man's reach again. The chain-mail would be a problem.

Twee observed his opponent while staying just out of sword reach. The blow had shaken the guardsman a bit, and he was moving slower. Twee looked for a weakness in the chain-mail. The links didn't close under the arms. For mobility, and perhaps for heat, there was a gap in the chain in the underarm area.

Twee dodged another blow. He had to do something quickly, or the man would corner him somewhere in the room.

He waited for a second when the guardsman was recovering from a swing of his sword. Then he darted inside the man's reach again and sank his tooth into the gap in the chain-mail under the man's arm.

The knife sank to its hilt into the guardsman's chest and then was jerked from Twee's grasp as the man pulled away from him.

Twee rose to his feet, unarmed, and faced the guardsman. The man started to step toward Twee with the tooth protruding sideways from his chest. Then he dropped his sword, dropped to his knees, and fell face forward to the ground.

# TIGER

# 1

Twee stood for a second, breathing heavily, then stepped over to the guardsman. He kicked the sword away, leaned over the man, and checked for a pulse. It was there. Ragged, but not gone.

Twee turned the man over. He pulled a handkerchief from his pocket, drew his knife out of the man's chest, wadded the kerchief up, and stuffed it into the wound to stop the bleeding. He wiped the dagger on the man's tabard.

The three men in the hall were all dead. The king's guardsman slumped against the wall might not have been at the beginning of the fight, but he was now.

Twee looked both ways down the corridor. There was no one in sight. The smell of smoke was still in the air but didn't seem close. He had no idea what to do next.

Then it occurred to him that there was only one choice. He headed down the corridor toward Vix's room.

The corridor was high enough in the castle that it had windows. Small ones and far between, but the morning sunlight was streaming in, and the contrast between the bloody scene behind Twee, the smell of smoke in the air, and the warm, bright light left him a little light-headed.

He walked cautiously down the hall. There was no one in sight and nothing to hear, but he didn't want anything to surprise him again, like when his door crashed open.

There was a rustling in the air at one side of the corridor ahead of him. Vix appeared out of nowhere. She ran to him and grabbed onto him like a drowning soul seizing a floating barrel.

"Twee," she said. "I was worried about you."

"I was worried about *you*," said Twee.

"What are we going to do?" said Vix. She looked anxious

but seemed otherwise all right.

"I don't know," said Twee. He thought for a moment. His first consideration had been to find Vix. He hadn't thought of what came after.

"Bear," he said, "and Anne. The guards will be busy, and they can help us figure out what to do."

Twee worried about the countess, but she had her guardsmen, and Bear and Anne were alone.

Vix grabbed Twee's hand and pulled him off down the corridor. She started spreading out her cobweb cloak.

There was no one in the dungeon guard post. The guardsmen had other priorities today. Vix went over to a row of keys that hung on the wall and took one.

On the way to the dungeon, they ran into several guardsmen. Initially, some in the countess's yellow, then later in the king's men's blue. They avoided them all, crouching under Vix's cloak until they passed.

Twee raced on ahead toward the door to Bear's cell. Vix followed with the key. When they reached the door, Twee called out to the window. "Bear, it's me, Twee."

Vix fumbled with the key a bit as Twee waited impatiently.

When the door opened, Bear stepped carefully out into the corridor. He blinked at the light. Twee grabbed him and pulled him into a hug. Bear seemed much healthier than he had when Twee saw him last.

"What's going on, Twee?" he said. "Where are the guards?"

Twee had planned to ask Bear what he thought they should do, but he didn't feel the need anymore. He knew what they had to do. He told Bear instead.

"Bear," he said. "This is Vix. We have to get Anne. The Lion's attacking. My grandfather was heir..."

Twee stopped. "There's too much, and we don't have time. I'll condense it."

"Bear," he tried again, "we need to help the countess. The

guys in blue are the bad guys, and the guys in yellow are our friends."

He turned to Vix. "Vix, do you know which cells the rest of the Raven's men are in?"

## 2

Twee led a small group of armed men through the King's Seat corridors toward the women's dungeon. The group included the Raven's men and two of the countess's guardsmen they had encountered. The countess's guardsmen recognized Twee immediately and were happy to follow him. One of them dropped to one knee when Twee started speaking to him.

Bear looked at Twee curiously when this happened. Twee pulled the man to his feet and led the group on.

The guard post at the women's dungeon was slightly better guarded than the men's was. There was one guardsman there in his blue tabard. When he saw ten armed men charge into the room, he dropped his sword immediately. Vix located the key for Anne's cell.

When Anne stepped out of her cell, Twee had difficulty seeing her face through the cloudiness that blurred his vision. It was the same face, however. There might have been a few gray hairs around the temples that weren't there before. There was undoubtedly some dungeon soot smearing her cheeks. But, this was the same face, the same voice that read to him until he fell asleep, which had taught him to speak. If Misha was his wolf mother, Anne had mothered the human in him.

Anne was even wearing the same blue smock he remembered, though it had suffered from its time in the dungeon.

The reasons there was a women's dungeon and that the Raven wasn't with them were fundamentally the same. The King's Seat was so massive there were, in total, eight different dungeon or prison facilities. There was no reason not to have a separate dungeon for the women, the men, and the more critical prisoners with so many options.

Anne took a weapon from the guard post. Then, the group turned to Twee to see what they should do next.

There was no hesitation.

"Vix," said Twee. "Can you lead us to the Aven Court?"

The Aven Court was the courtyard below Twee's window, where he had seen the beginnings of a pitched battle between the countess's men and the regent's. It felt an eternity ago, but it couldn't have been more than a few hours.

With Vix and Twee in the lead, the group raced through the corridors again.

The corridors were largely clear. They encountered and recruited one more of the countess's guards before reaching the wide double doors leading out into the Aven Court.

Bear took the lead as they strode up to the double doors. He threw them open, and the group stepped out into the courtyard. The battle was still on.

The most direct access to the Emerald Wing was through the court. That was where the regent was attacking. Twee learned from the countess's guardsmen that the regent had concluded the countess was the ringleader in a plot against him.

Along with his other moves to ease his path to the throne, the regent sent men to arrest or kill the countess.

Bear, Twee, Anne, Vix, and their assembled men charged into the court. The regent's men were forcing the remnants of the guardsmen who were guarding the court back through the doors into the Ruby Wing.

Twee's force came into the courtyard from the opposite side, directly behind the regent's forces.

Twee had picked up a sword from one of the guardrooms. It seemed a more appropriate weapon for the day.

Twee raised his sword and charged at the men in the blue tabards.

"For the countess D'Arilo!" he cried.

# 3

The regent's guardsmen were not expecting the countess's men to receive reinforcements and certainly weren't expecting an attack from behind. Seeing what was happening, the countess's men surged forward with renewed vigor. What was a row of blue-clad soldiers pressing back a line of yellow-clad ones turned into a disorganized brawl of individual duels and scuffles.

Twee immediately lost track of where everyone was except for the few soldiers right next to him. He glimpsed Vix disappearing at one point and felt a great relief.

Time faded into a blur. Twee couldn't think about anything other than his immediate surroundings for the next eternity. It might have been five minutes. It might have been an hour. He had to focus every thought on making sure no one was striking at him from behind or on either side.

He had enough time, between breaths, to reconsider the wisdom of his charge. He still didn't have any armor, and these men were better equipped and perhaps better prepared than he was.

The smells and sounds of the battle absorbed Twee. He darted from here to there, trying his best to help the Raven's and the countess's men while keeping himself alive.

He got a few blows in and managed to avoid injury. When all is said and done, one of the greatest victories in a battle is being able to walk away alive and uninjured.

When things quieted, and the last of the blue-clad men was either lying on the ground or taken prisoner, Twee looked around himself. The countess's guardsmen were checking their wounded and trying to restore order. Bear and Anne stood over one of the Raven's men who had fallen during the battle. Vix seemed to have come up with another bottle of her 'Mama's Spit' potion and was ministering to the wounded.

The captain of the countess's guardsmen approached Twee.

He knelt and spoke quietly.

"Your Majesty," he said, "Thank you for your timely aid. This battle might have had a different result without you and your men. I believe the countess will want to see you. Can I escort you to her?"

Bear and Anne were within hearing range and exchanged an astonished glance at this speech.

Twee, mostly embarrassed, gathered them, Vix, and the Raven's men and followed the captain up the stairs.

As they stepped into the countess's drawing-room, which seemed to have become a focal point for planning, the countess's gentleman usher looked at them and just sighed. He seemed to give up on announcing the whole group and instead just picked out what he saw as the most important.

"His Majesty, King Twilight!"

The countess turned toward the door and called out, "Twee!" in a relieved voice. Then she flushed, faced toward Twee, gave a graceful curtsy, and said in more measured tones, "I'm relieved to see you, Your Majesty. I feared the worst when we found the guards outside your door dead this morning."

The room was much changed from how it had looked the day before. There was a large table in the middle with a chart of the King's Seat spread out on it. There were wooden blocks on the map in various colors, representing the forces of nobles and the regent. Messengers and couriers were coming and going. Several of the guardsmen from the battle below had already made their way up here.

Twee felt a flush of his own creeping up his collar. He wasn't used to this much attention. And the references to "King Twilight" and "Your Majesty" made him extremely uncomfortable. Regardless, he stepped forward to the table with the map on it and tried to take in the situation that the blocks displayed.

The captain of the countess's guard bowed to the countess and gestured toward Twee, Bear, Anne, and the rest of the Raven's men. "Your ladyship, the young king, and his allies made the difference in the courtyard below. Without them, I wouldn't be here.

"His Grace himself fought valiantly. Some of the men were saying he fought like a tiger."

The countess smiled. "When this is all over, then, I guess we'll need to change the symbol on the tabards of the king's guard."

## 4

Now that the courtyard was clear, the countess sent messengers out to all the allies she had courted over the last few years. The regent wasn't well-liked. Once she convinced a noble or dignitary that Twee was who she said he was, winning their allegiance to his cause was not hard.

As Twee studied it, the map displayed a picture that did not look favorable for the regent. There was an island of blue in the middle, surrounded by a rainbow of other colors.

"We've been waiting for him to make the first move," said the countess. "Some of our allies are more comfortable arresting him for starting a coup than they were with starting action against him.

"In addition to his attack on me, he tried to gain forceful control of the high court and attacked several others he felt betrayed him. I think he seriously underestimated how many of the lords of the land were arrayed against him."

"I'm uncomfortable with the King Twilight stuff," said Twee.

"I'm sorry, Your Majesty," said the countess with a wink. "When the old king died, the regency officially ended, and you became king, even without a coronation. You are the king, regardless of what you, or the former regent, want."

The drawing-room became a focal point for the organization of the battle against the regent. Messengers came and went. Each message brought about the rearrangement of the pieces on the map. It seemed foreordained that the regent didn't have a chance from early on. The forces arraigned against him were too overwhelming.

Twee tried to help plan and coordinate the messages and

movement of soldiers. The countess had been preparing for this day for a while. She seemed to have a mind for strategy, so Twee limited his help to suggestions and recommendations.

He was glad to realize that his time in court and meeting the various nobles and the other dignitaries hadn't been wasted. He recognized the names, colors, and symbols of most of the pieces on the map.

At some point, when there was a break in the action, Twee took Bear, Anne, and the other Raven's men aside and filled them in. Anne and Twee hadn't had a chance to talk, as there hadn't been a free moment.

She gushed about how big he had grown. He told her about Vix. Vix stood shyly off to one side of the group. Twee pulled her forward to introduce her to them.

Bear was the one who brought up the big unspoken question.

"So, what's with all this 'Your Majesty' stuff?"

"Apparently," said Twee, "I'm the grandson of the former heir to the throne. The old king just died, so I'm going to be the next king."

"Well, that's big news," said Bear.

"Why didn't you say something when you lived with us?" said Anne.

"I didn't know," said Twee.

At the end of the day, the sunset light streaming into the drawing-room from the westward-facing windows lit the room with a reddish glow. A messenger arrived with the news that the regent had been captured and arrested. His remaining men had surrendered.

The captain of the countess's guard, who had helped Twee and the countess direct the various allied forces' strategy, led the assembled people in the room in a chant.

"All hail our good king Twilight," he called out.

"Hip, Hip, Hooray!"

"Hip, Hip, Hooray!"

# 5

The morning after the battle of King's Seat, as it came to be known, Twee woke up in his familiar bed in the room he had lived in for the past year, for the last time. Things had ended on a chaotic note the evening before, and they hadn't had time to set up new, more appropriate quarters for him. Twee was just as glad. If he had his way, this would remain his quarters indefinitely. Still, he imagined he might not get his way on this one.

He awoke with the feeling he had forgotten something. *The Raven*, he thought with a sudden rush of guilt and embarrassment. He ran to the door in his nightshirt.

Two guards were stationed outside, dressed in the countess's yellow.

"There was a prisoner," said Twee, "the Raven. They were keeping him in the regent's special prisoner dungeon. He may have been freed, or not, last night. I need to see him."

"Your Grace," said one guard and headed off down the corridor.

Twee dressed. They hadn't had time to prepare him a new wardrobe, as he imagined they might, and it comforted him to get dressed in his familiar clothes. He put his tooth into his boot sheath and wondered how long it would be before they tried to take that away from him.

There was a knock on the door. When Twee opened it, two new guards stood there, leading the Raven. He was still chained. Apparently, the word he should be freed hadn't gotten out. Twee realized that word had to come from him.

Unexpectedly, Bear was with them. He had thrown one of the tabards of the countess's guardsmen over his clothes. The countess's guards were very grateful to Bear, Anne, and the rest of the men who had helped them in the battle of Aven Court. Apparently, Bear was now an honorary guardsman.

"I tried to tell them to remove his chains," said Bear, "but they wouldn't listen to me."

"Remove his chains immediately," said Twee.

The guardsmen moved a little slowly but did so.

To Twee, the Raven looked much like he had when he was first brought before the regent. His hair was just as dark, he stood as proudly, his cuts and bruises had healed, but he looked a little thinner. He looked up into Twee's eyes, inclined his head, and said, "Your Grace."

Twee, Bear, and the Raven talked for an hour. Not too long after they began, there was a knock on the door with an urgent request for the king to start his official day. But Twee had already learned that being king meant people would listen to him when he said something. He told them to wait until the meeting was done, and they did.

The Raven shared Bear's feeling of responsibility for Twee's capture by the king's men so many years ago. He was the one who had requested Twee participate in the mission that had ended badly.

Twee asked about the different views of the Raven's calling. Was he a freedom fighter battling against the regent's oppressive taxation or just an outlaw?

The truth, of course, as it always is, was somewhere in between.

# 6

Twee was in the throne room for the first time as king. There were formalities and rules for how everything was done. He spent a great deal of time trying to learn what to do and how to do the things they told him, the way they told him. He hadn't been able to think much about decision-making.

The current task at hand was forming a cabinet and selecting advisers. People filled the room. All of them had some interest in what his decisions would be. Several of the ministers who had been part of the regent's cabinet and his former chief minister were there. The countess had filled Twee in on which ministers could be trusted and which he should avoid. Some who were more deeply immersed in the regent's plans had been arrested.

The Raven was there, with Bear, Anne, and Vix. Twee wanted to ensure he had as many friendly faces in the room as possible.

There were crowds of nobles and dignitaries, all wanting to see and speak with the new king. Twee recognized many faces but didn't feel like he knew any of them.

The countess insisted she didn't want a position in Twee's cabinet. She was on hand to help him get established. But, she had her own obligations, and being part of the king's cabinet wasn't one of them.

The countess told him the regent's former first minister, Lord Taedum, could be of service. He had played both sides, leading up to the coup, to a certain degree. But he had been very helpful to her. In addition, he had a wealth of valuable knowledge and information about the kingdom and the court.

Twee was sitting on the throne. It wasn't very comfortable. He was told a coronation was essential and would happen soon. It wasn't to confirm his authority but to celebrate it.

"Lord Taedum," said Twee, "can I appoint a new governor to Grisput?"

"Your Grace," said Lord Taedum. "The Governorship of Grisput is a hereditary role.

"The position of king's envoy to Grisput," Lord Taedum continued, "is an appointed post. And, an influential one."

"Thank you, your Lordship," said Twee. "I would like to have someone go to Grisput and do two things for me."

"What would those things be?" said Lord Taedum.

"I would like someone to locate a bondsman named Reynard and bring him here."

"Very well, Your Grace, and the other?"

"A living stipend for a woman named Maria Wodenswold. She lives in the craftsman's district."

"It shall be done," said Lord Taedum. "And as to selecting your cabinet, ministers, and advisers?"

"I have my advisers right here," said Twee. He swept his hand out in a gesture covering Vix, Anne, Bear, and the Raven.

# 7

Twee tried to fill his voice with authority. "Cousin," he said, "You have caused grave harm to the kingdom of Liamec with your policies and actions, but I am inclined to be merciful."

"'We are inclined...', Your Grace," whispered Lord Taedum urgently.

"I am inclined to be merciful," repeated Twee.

"You can take your mercy and stick it where the sun doesn't shine," said the Lion.

Twee stood on the last step of the dais below the throne. The Lion stood before him with his hands manacled behind his back. The Lion was between two guardsmen, each of whom had a grip on one of his arms. He wasn't kneeling. The guards had been about to force him to kneel, but Twee had waved them off.

The Lion still cut quite a figure. Even dirty and ill-kempt from a stay in a dungeon cell, his mane tangled and begrimed, he nonetheless looked like a man to be admired.

With a few exceptions, the scene was a mirror of when Twee was brought before the Lion.

"You have to have him executed," the Raven said. "It was treason. An attempt at a military coup. Even if you don't consider the years of tyranny."

"Executions," said Twee, "will not mark my reign.

"What are we going to do with you?" he continued, tilting his head to one side and gazing at the Lion.

Twee's court had been forming. Vix stood just above him on the dais. She had taken her riding outfit and modified it even a little more. The part below the waist was almost trouser-like. The countess had informed her it was a bit scandalous and would turn some heads, but that was how fashions began, and perhaps she would start a new trend. (It was, of course, filled with pockets, both visible and hidden.)

The guardsmen were wearing their new blue king's men tabards. The silhouette of the lion's head had been replaced. There was a discussion, and the conclusion was reached that the lion was too closely associated with the regent. The countess had suggested the silhouette of a tiger's head.

Twee had opted instead for a black silhouette of a wolf's head.

The Raven, and all his men, were pardoned. They were being considered heroic freedom fighters against the oppression of the prince regent, not outlaws.

Anne was not in court. Twee had asked her what she wanted.

Anne told Twee what she wanted, more than anything, was an escorted trip to a small mill house in a village somewhere in the southeastern corner of his kingdom. She had left a few days ago. Bear led her escort in his new capacity as captain of the king's guard.

The Raven was becoming one of Twee's chief advisers. Twee asked him for advice on many matters, especially military issues and strategy questions. Twee didn't always take his advice, as with his suggestion for the regent, but he always considered it.

Reynard had come to Capitol and gone already. Twee appointed him king's envoy to Grisput, and they had a long discussion about the king's wishes for his envoy. The bondage system was deeply ingrained in the economic system of the city. The independent city-state would probably go to war before giving it up. They discussed ways to improve things for bondys and ways to steer the city toward more substantial changes.

Twee sent off a few of the former Raven's men with the mission of locating Oscar. He wanted them to inform him of the pardon and invite him to Capitol if he was still alive.

Twee looked the Lion straight in the eye. "Cousin," he said, "I don't know what to do with you. Give me a little time, and I'll come up with something."

He made a gesture to the guards, and they left the throne room, leading the Lion between them.

Twee looked to Lord Taedum, who nodded and stepped forward.

"The court of the King's Bench is no longer in session. All rise for the king."

Twee stepped back up the dais and offered his arm to Vix. He was exhausted. The interview with the Lion was the last case of a very long court day. Vix took his arm, and they strode together down the scarlet carpet toward the door.

As they walked down the carpet arm in arm, the setting sun shone through the westward-facing windows, raising coppery glints in Vix's hair. Twee stood straight and proud. Perhaps he hadn't reached his full height, but he was almost there, and he already stood as tall as most men. And if he wasn't as tall as some, as they say, kingship adds at least two inches.

He had refused a crown and tried to keep the new wardrobe they made for him as simple as possible.

Even so, there wasn't one person who looked at him that didn't see the figure of a king.

Twee stumbled. Perhaps it was the exhaustion he felt. Maybe it was a crease in the carpet. He stumbled and might have fallen if Vix hadn't tightened her grip on his arm.

Twee turned, smiled at her, and the two of them walked out the door together.

# EPILOGUE

If the story of the land of Liamec hadn't been lost. If the lives and struggles of the citizens of the country between the blue mountains and the peaks known as the Etenies hadn't been omitted from the annals of time. If the lineage of the kings and queens of Liamec hadn't been mislaid by the scribes and historians.

Then, certainly, the twilight years would have been recorded as the best years in the kingdom's history.

Dear Reader,

I hope you've enjoyed *The Wolf's Tooth*. If so, you will probably enjoy *By the Sea*, the next *Tale of Liamec*.

Also, if you are curious about who Twilight's parents are, then you might want to consider reading *The Channeler Trilogy*. Twilight's birth and separation from his parents are described in that series.

If you enjoyed the story, I hope you'll consider dropping a quick review on Amazon,

Thank you for reading!

# BOOKS IN THIS SERIES

*The tales of Liamec*

## By The Sea

A young woman.
A perilous game of wits.
And a destiny that challenges the gods...

In the gray fishing village of Chelle by the Sea, Annabelle's life has been defined by the ebb and flow of the ocean and the weight of her brother's tragic demise. But when an enigmatic nobleman on a white horse arrives, everything changes.

Llyr, a stranger to both the villagers and Annabelle, brings a proposition that could alter her destiny. As they embark on an epic journey together, Annabelle must decipher Llyr's true intentions. Can she trust him with her life, or does he have his own hidden agenda?

In the spellbinding standalone second installment of the Tales of Liamec series, By the Sea, J. Steven Lamperti weaves a tapestry of magic, intrigue, and betrayal. Follow Annabelle and Llyr as they navigate treacherous waters, facing unimaginable obstacles and the wrath of the gods.

Discover a captivating tale of courage, friendship, and the ultimate test of wits. Join Annabelle and Llyr on their perilous quest that will challenge everything they believe in. Experience the enchanting world of Liamec in this unforgettable YA fantasy adventure.

## Twilight's Fall

A young king, new to his realm.
His men slaughtered in a devastating ambush.
The kingdom's fate hangs on a sword's edge...

As trust shatters and betrayal lurks among his allies, Twilight, the young king of Liamec, must place his faith in the loyalty of those beside him. He and a few survivors embark on a treacherous journey back to the capital. His motley group of companions all rise to the occasion in ways he never expects. The young guardsman, Corentin, especially, has a mysterious secret power that may prove pivotal.

But safety eludes them, for the traitor has turned many of the land's nobles against their king. Reluctantly, Twilight must confront the looming prospect of a war against his own people, risking everything to save his kingdom, protect his queen Vix, and preserve his own life.

If the final battle arrives, will Corentin's mystical, hidden connection to the underworld hold the key to their salvation, or will this be Twilight's Fall, heralding the end of the kingdom of Liamec?

In J. Steven Lamperti's spellbinding tale of magic, treachery, and breathtaking battles, join King Twilight and his companions on an unmissable journey. Twilight's Fall is an epic YA fantasy novel that will sweep you into a world of thrilling adventure and pulse-pounding suspense. Grab your sword, stand alongside King Twilight, and prepare for an unforgettable battle that will shape the destiny of an entire kingdom.

## The Pirates Of Meara

A city built on stolen treasures.
Dark secrets and hidden truths.
Escaping Meara's cold-blooded pirates is their only hope...

Meara, a glistening pirate city adorned in turquoise and gold, holds deadly secrets. Mouse, a street-smart wharf rat with a mysterious power concealed behind a dirty eye patch, becomes an unlikely hero when he rescues Fern, the captivating daughter of a duke, from ruthless pirates. Together, they must navigate treacherous alleys, outsmart Bluebeard, the pirate lord pursuing them, and uncover enigmatic truths to reunite Fern with her father.

Time is running out, and the shadows of Meara grow darker. Betrayal lurks at every corner, testing their fragile trust as they fight for survival. They delve deeper, unearthing secrets buried beneath the city's streets and hiding under the vast expanse of the sea. Will Bluebeard catch Mouse and Fern before they can escape beneath the ocean's waves?

Embark on an unforgettable voyage with The Pirates of Meara, a thrilling standalone tale in J. Steven Lamperti's acclaimed Tales of Liamec fantasy series.

# BOOKS BY THIS AUTHOR

## Moon & Shadow

A young farmer.
An unexpected gift.
And powerful, deadly magic from the heavens...

One fateful evening in a quiet medieval village, Sebastian reaches up and pulls the moon down from the sky. As he sets off to market the next day, he discovers he can borrow mystical gifts from his fellow villagers: the delicate shadows of his true love's feet, the smelly wind of a dog's breath, the village fool's simplicity, and an arrogant man's brittle self-esteem.

When a terrifying monster attacks his village, the girl Anise, a survivor of the beast's assault on a neighboring town, helps Sebastian use the moon and his borrowed gifts as armor — turning the simple farm boy into the Knight of Moon & Shadow.

With Anise's help, Sebastian realizes it's up to him to protect his home from powerful enemies and safeguard the ones he loves. But on the treacherous path ahead, he must face the spirits of death, confront the shadows in his own soul, and navigate the enigmatic moon spirit, Luna.

If the Knight of Moon & Shadow can't destroy the source of the nightmare beasts, it'll be the end for his village and everyone he loves...

Moon & Shadow is the first book in J. Steven Lamperti's Channeler Trilogy. It's an enchanting YA Fantasy with sweet romance, quirky characters, and engaging humor. The unforgettable epic tale continues in Sun & Dream.

## Sun & Dream

Anise's dreams are not just figments of her imagination; they are a source of immense power she can barely control.

When her uncle, Sebastian, takes Anise from their simple farming village to the Academy, a wizard's school on the other side of Liamec, they embark on a perilous journey.

And once they reach the Academy, Anise's power attracts attention from more than just her family and teachers. The Watcher, a malevolent presence that she senses in her dreams, seeks to use her power for nefarious purposes. And why is Helios, the sun god, protecting her?

As Anise grapples with everyday challenges like an old crush resurfacing, making friends, and excelling in her classes, she also faces more significant problems: Her dreams hold a formidable power, she is haunted by the enigmatic Watcher, and she discovers the signs of a sinister conspiracy.

As Anise battles to control her abilities, a dark danger, present since the Academy's inception, looms, jeopardizing reality and the very existence of Liamec.

Sun & Dream, the captivating second installment of The Channeler Trilogy by J. Steven Lamperti weaves a tale of magic, danger, and self-discovery that will keep you on the edge of your seat.

## Death & Dragon

Trapped in the realm of dream and nightmare, will Anise wake up to save the land of Liamec from dragons and dream storms?

Anise has finished training in the magical arts at the Academy, the school where the wizards of Liamec learn to control their powers. But, one of the school's masters, the villainous Lorenzo, has banished her to the realm of dreams, trapping her there. When she finally wakes from her years of dreaming, the Kingdom of Liamec has changed.

Dragons are raiding the northern parts of the kingdom. Dream storms shake the fabric of the land. Anise is still being hunted by Lorenzo's nightmare beasts, twins to the ones her uncle fought in the village of Hero long ago. Can Anise stop the storms, brave the dangers, and save the kingdom?

In the sweeping conclusion to the award-winning Channeler Trilogy, J Steven Lamperti wraps up the threads spun in the earlier books.

Anise must return to the realm of dream, defeat Lorenzo, outmaneuver the dragons, and rescue Liamec from certain doom!

Printed in Poland
by Amazon Fulfillment
Poland Sp. z o.o., Wrocław

38609905R00136